THE TWELVE RINGS

Grant Crockett

Dedication

This book is dedicated to my writing critique group, the Future Authors; it is also dedicated to the Horizon Jaguars. Long may they reign.

I would also like to thank my editors, Colin Snider and Carrie Crockett, as well as my reading tutor, Pam Carlson, who inspires me to write and read.

About the Author

Grant Crockett is a middle-school student who lives in Kearney, Nebraska. He has two sisters and two brothers.

Grant's writing career began in second grade when he began to write short stories for pleasure. The first character Grant brought to life was Nick Baker, who also appears in this novel.

The author would like to encourage all young writers to courageously express themselves through writing. "When you write," he has said, "it's not because you want to, but because you have to." Some of the works that have inspired him are *The Chronicles of Narnia*, *I am Number Four*, *Charlie Bone,* and *The Michael Vey* series. He also enjoys Stephen Miller's *Captain Justo*.

Table of Contents

Introduction: 12

Chapter One: Jonathan: 24

Chapter Two: Isabelle: 37

Chapter Three: Lina: 43

Chapter Four: Michael: 49

Chapter Five: Tom: 55

Chapter Six: Charlie: 62

Chapter Seven: Quincy: 73

Chapter Eight: Landon: 84

Chapter Nine: Marcus: 93

Chapter Ten: Ashley: 107

Chapter Eleven: Nick: 115

Chapter Twelve: Rebecca: 124

Chapter Thirteen: The Horn: 131

Chapter Fourteen: The Dream: 136

Chapter Fifteen: The Portal: 145

Chapter Sixteen: The Shruut: 150

Chapter Seventeen:
Twelve Doors: 155

Chapter Eighteen:
Six Not Three: 162

Chapter Nineteen:
Thirteen Portals: 172

Chapter Twenty:
The Twelve Chairs: 178

Introduction to Volume II: 192

Introduction

The History of the Twelve--the History of Renmell

January, February, March, April, May, June, July, August, September, October, November, and December. These words refer to the months of the year, or so they say. But, even before dinosaurs ruled the earth, before history as we know it began, another group of humans governed the planet, and it was these who coined the twelve names of the months. To this group of advanced humans, the names were more than words by which segments of time were called; they were really ciphers that denoted special powers.

No one has ever written about these early inhabitants of Earth before; until now, no one has ever known their story. The closest any human came to stumbling onto the true history of the Earth was Julius Caesar. His scribes discovered some ancient records upon which the twelve names were inscribed. Thus, he "borrowed," or actually stole, the names of the months, making them his own. The story that follows is a factual history of what the books in school will never tell you. What follows is the truth.

The first people on earth were not unlike the soldiers of the Roman Empire; they were colonists and soldiers who came to our planet with conquest on their minds. The most powerful of these were representatives of a cosmic empire that was ever expanding: it was called the Ranian Empire, an unfortunately dark civilization full of greed and evil.

The primary enemy of the Ranik was yet another group of advanced humans, the Ellmarikaih, who ruled a sizable portion of the universe. The Ranik found our planet attractive and hospitable, and settled on the large landmass, Pangaea, which today we vaguely remember only in shreds of myth.

Other nations, however, had already settled on Earth and had progressed technologically. Some of them had discovered gunpowder and had built up militaries similar to those of the World War I era.

The Ranian soldiers, however, were much more advanced than any of those on Earth. Just one of their rookie soldiers, having been dropped into a city of seven million inhabitants, single-handedly took it over in a space of four hours. He had worn a battle suit capable of shielding him from anything that could be thrown or shot; he had carried no more than a single pistol, but the weapon was so technologically sophisticated that it could take down an entire skyscraper with one blast. Not surprisingly, about half of the people of earth surrendered quickly and joined the Ranian Empire.

Those who did not surrender perished, and those who had surrendered were eventually ordered to leave but refused. The Ranik then destroyed their cities and enslaved those few who were left—the rich and the poor, the healthy and the infirm, male and female. Imprisoned in the ruins of their cities, the survivors were fed little and told nothing. Government military patrolled these last stragglers from the skies, gathering intelligence as they hovered above the decimated cities in helicopter-life crafts.

Time went by, and the people became hungry for change. They began to fight back. They captured some of the choppers and used them to further their cause, the people's revolution, otherwise known as the Battle for Freedom.

Although the war lasted for two full decades, at its conclusion, the people remained defeated. When the Ranian leadership decided to abandon Earth as a colony, they ordered all the enslaved back into space (approximately eighty-eight percent of the population). The authorities never found the other twelve percent of their subjects, for they had disappeared beneath the earth into hiding, surviving in spaces the government could not imagine. Nearly seventy thousand resisters hid, battled for their lives for eight long years, and survived after the government left. These strong ones then formed a new nation: Renmell.

Renmell's founders remembered the twelve long years they had spent underground, struggling to survive. They resolved to respect and remember that twelve-year period of time prior to their nation's birth. To this end, they divided time itself into twelve segments and called them months. Yes, the segments of time that we use today still bear the names of the Renmellion months; somehow, through the changing ages, the words survived up until the present.

We use the names of the months now without knowing their true meanings or their origin. This ancient historical account will show, however, that these words were also symbols for uncommon and special powers.

Just when things seemed to be quieting down for the Renmellians, a new species came into view: the dinosaur. The origin of the dinosaur has survived to this day. During the war, a man and his wife had sailed to Storia Island seeking safety. There they grew sick, having caught a disease that altered their forms. They morphed into dinosaurs.

Time passed. Storia Island became populated with dinosaurs that were fond of attacking explorer-sailors who tried to visit their island. Once, a few of the braver explorer-sailors fought back, killing seven of the dinosaurs. Then they desperately fled to the beaches using laser shotguns as a form of last defense.

The sailors launched their boat into the sea in what seemed like the nick of time. Though they believed they were safe, they were not. Unbeknownst to all, a very small dinosaur had crawled aboard their skiff under cover of darkness. She had laid her eggs in corners. The sailors found and killed her, but she had already left behind a dangerous legacy persevered in the form of hatching eggs.

Baby dinosaurs multiplied, spread, became strong, and infested the land. They attacked the town of Ream in the state of Frendall and killed every resident within it. As news of the massacre at Ream spread, the people of Frendall grew angry. They grabbed their weapons and headed off to war, a war that would last three long years. Again, the dinosaurs triumphed.

As Frendall collapsed in chaos around them, the government's leaders resolved to preserve sacred things and keep them safe. Taking a sacred ring, the ring of Frendall, they descended down long passageways which took them deep below the city to a storeroom of ancient, special weapons: the sacred sword, the shield, wand, bow, knife, and spear. As Frendall fell, the ring, the symbol of its power, endured. It ended up in the possession of King Jelms who resided at the nation's capital, Zanthar.

During the following year, other states resolved to follow Frendall's lead. They passed their rings to King Jelms, who hid them in an underground cave. Then, realizing they would fall and the end was probably near, all remaining kingdoms came together and joined King Jelms in battle.

The troops marched to the forest where Frendall had once been. Although sixteen thousand people waged war on the dinosaurs, only three hundred returned to Zanthar. The King himself perished in the battle; the army fled.

Imagining that they would be safe within the ruins of Zanthar, the survivors built a last monument, a glass-roofed structure with steel walls. Here, for nine years, they lived in a state of uneasy peace while industriously building weapons and creating potions.

But, one day, at noon, the piercing screech of a Pterodactyl echoed throughout Zanthar. The glass roof instantly shattered and broke. Its shards fell, from which ninety perished. Then, more Pterodactyls darkened the skies above the city, attacking and killing six hundred people. Within ten minutes only twenty guards out of one hundred twenty were living. Disaster had struck once again.

As the slaughter raged, three brothers found themselves being led down an underground path. Far beneath the capital building, down into the caves of Jelms, beyond the boundaries of their known world, the three journeyed. Above ground, Zanthar fell for the last time; but, miles below the earth the brothers were ordained to be the last guardians of the kingdom's powers. Each was given one of the twelve original rings and a potion: together, they drank. The liquid altered their bodies, making them impervious to disease and aging. Unless injured by the hand of another, the brothers could not die.

After Zanthar fell, they--Menzi, Loonce, and Merk—devised a plan. Menzi was the eldest of the three. He was deeply tanned, his head covered with curly, black hair, and he possessed a penetrating gaze.

"We are now immortal and here is what we must do," he told his brothers. "We must put a spell on ourselves that will cause us to remain frozen—as if in suspended animation—until the time is right for us to pass the rings to the next guardians."

"But why wait? We are immortals," Loonce, the second eldest brother, asked. His head was bald and his eyes brown and earnest.

"Because we ourselves do not know when the time will be right," Menzi said. "It could be many hundreds of years. We must rely on the rings, and allow their powers to reawaken us when we are needed."

"You are right, frozen we must be," Loonce agreed.

And that was that. The brothers cast a spell of reversible freezing upon themselves, knowing that they might be in for a long wait.

As their scribe, I have remained with the three brothers Menzi, Loonce, and Merk these many years, and I have recorded their doings until this moment. With them now frozen, I remain absolutely alone, the last citizen of a fallen nation. My own death will soon come. Timelessness awaits.

Chapter One
Jonathan

At the time of the spell and the freezing, the brothers they had no idea how long they would remain in suspended animation. The rings decided, however, that during the last few months of 1999, they should reenter the world of the living, and search for the twelve young humans who would bear the rings of power. The first of these to be found was Jonathan.

The date was January 1st, 2000. Menzi, Loonce, and Merk had been unfrozen a few months before, and now worked as mechanics. After witnessing the fall of Frendall and surviving numerous wars, the brothers found the work to be extraordinarily easy, even pleasant. They spent their free time reading books of all types and watching ESPN, which portrayed conflicts of an especially tame and entertaining nature.

On this particular January day, however, the three waited anxiously in a hospital corridor. Their excitement level was high, for the rings had suggested to them that the first of the twelve chosen ring bearers was about to enter the world. They were about to give the first of the twelve rings to the very first baby.

"Is there anything we can do for the mother?" Menzi fretted, grimacing. "It's all so scary."

"How should we know? We're not even in the delivery room." Loonce paced nervously. "Plus, they'd never let us in. What do we know about such things?"

Suddenly, they saw the doors to the operating room swing open. The doctor emerged, sorrow and weariness on his face. The brothers approached him.

"How is the baby? Healthy? Can you give us any news?" Menzi asked, hoping that they would be taken to be part of the family. The doctor sighed and then spoke.

"The child's mother died during the delivery, but the baby is fine. As you doubtless know, his father perished in a car crash a few months ago, so the baby is now an orphan. No other relatives or family exist, unless you are relations and would like to take him. Otherwise, we have no choice but to put him up for adoption. I do hate to see such a beautiful little baby go into the foster system." The doctor frowned. "The woman's final words to her baby were, 'Jonathan, I love you.' Apparently it was his father's name. Did you know him?"

The three shook their heads. Dr. Wilson turned away slowly. Menzi looked at Merk and Loonce. "Loonce, Merk, do we have a plan B?" he asked. They glanced at one another and sighed and smiled all at once.

"OK, fine, but remember that you are fully responsible for him," Loonce said. "Pure and simple—we're not changing any diapers or going to any parent-teacher conferences."

Menzi nodded, trying to hide the smile on his face, and looked toward the doctor. "Yes, I know, and I know what this all means: I must find a way to adopt the child at all costs."

Menzi ran after the doctor. "Dr. Wilson, would we be able to adopt Jonathan?"

"I couldn't tell you," the surgeon answered. "But if you think that you might really want to adopt him, and you are serious, go to the nursery. Someone there should be able to help you. It usually costs about five hundred dollars, but you do have a chance — to my knowledge no one else has come forward. But, in three days until he will be sent to a foster family, so you'll have to work fast." Smiling slightly now, the doctor strode off.

The immortals looked at each other, and saw that all their faces said the same thing: let's get ready.

THREE DAYS LATER

"We must get back to the hospital now!" Menzi and his three brothers sat in his house, planning. While his brothers lounged on the couch, a table with magazines as well as ancient books before them, Menzi hopped around the room in excitement.

"I have six thousand dollars in my pocket. That should be more than enough, right?"

"Probably, but you go, we're tired," Loonce said, sipping a coke and scrutinizing the golf tournament on ESPN. "Have fun."

"OK, you slackers — you sit here and I'll be back in an hour."

Menzi ran from the house and headed for the hospital in his truck. When he arrived, he pulled a sheaf of papers out of his pocket and went directly to the girl at the front desk.

Her name badge read, "How May I Help you? My name is Stephanie."

"Hey Steph, I know how you can help me: I'm here about an adoption," Menzi declared confidently, trying to hide his grin. "I would like to adopt the little baby named Jonathan Anderson who is in this very nursery!" He thumped the reception desk. The bold tone of Menzi's voice surprised even himself.

"I'm trying remember whether he's still here," Stephanie said vaguely, as if saying, what's in it for me? "And by the way, my name is not Steph, although . . ." At the sight of the one hundred dollar bill Menzi pushed across the desk toward her, she reconsidered and said, "Well, actually, I could probably answer to either name." She turned her head slightly and winked at Menzi, as if she had suddenly just recognized him as a long lost friend.

Steph jumped up and escorted Menzi down the hall. "This way to the nursery," she said. Her high heels clicked on the tile and she snapped her gum about every seven steps. "By the way, the whole adoption fee is one thousand dollars—are you good with that, fella?"

"One thousand dollars!" Menzi almost shouted.

"That's the price," Steph grinned.

"No, I'm good, I'm ready for anything," Menzi answered with more than a touch of bravado. He held up a packet of bills tied by a fraying blue string and handed it over to Steph, though a little unhappily.

Stuffing the wad into her pocket, Stephanie halted outside a door marked "nursery." She rapped on it softly. "Don't worry, I'll take care of the paper work," she said. "Good luck." She turned and clicked and snapped back down the hallway. What a noisy person, thought Menzi.

Menzi entered the dimly lit room. A row of babies lay in tiny bassinets against the wall, some crying, some sleeping, some just looking around or attempting to suck on their cute little fists. Menzi looked at each child, but had no problem finding Jonathan: only one of the babies had dark chocolaty eyes and skin the color of coffee. His hair was black.

Uttering a spell under his breath, Menzi looked into Jonathan's eyes, which widened as if he had something to tell Menzi as well. Carefully, Menzi removed the ring from his pocket and put it onto Jonathan's finger. "Handy that it adjusts to the wearer's size," he muttered, "and that only chosen ones can see it." It was true, only those who were associated with the Twelve, or the Twelve themselves, could see the rings.

"It's you," Menzi whispered happily to the baby. "It's really you. Do you know that you have almost bankrupted me?" He took the baby and held him gently.

"You will be able to speak soon. Do you understand?"

Jonathan seemed to nod.

"Good," Menzi said. "I see it has started already."

With Jonathan in his arms, Menzi felt a swell of pride and the smallest beginnings of parental love as he reentered his home and held the child up for his brothers to admire.

"How is he?" Merk asked. Menzi held the infant up in his arms. "Brother, he's perfect. Just great. And look, he's even asleep--I gave him the spell."

Loonce looked up from his book and shrieked. "What? You gave him the spell?"

"He will be better off with it!" Menzi said.

"Do you know what will happen now?" Loonce asked.

"You know what the Ellmarikaih told us," Menzi argued.

Loonce knew that he had lost. "Fair enough," he sighed. Together, they laid Jonathan in his crib. As soon as he was set down, the baby awoke and pried the bars apart, rendering the crib useless.

"He knows what to do, apparently," Merk said. "Smart kid." They took Jonathan out of his crib and put him on the ground. After a few minutes, he was walking up and down the halls and, a few minutes later, the stairs. They went outside, onto the grass in the front yard, and waited. This was the big test.

"This is it," said Merk. "Perhaps we will learn what his power is."

Jonathan looked around and then picked up some grass. He gripped it tightly in his hand, and the grass turned ash gray. The brothers stared at him.

"This is better than we thought." Loonce said, "the touch of death and telepathy."

Chapter Two
Isabelle

17 Years Later

Isabelle Dean was born on February 2nd, 2000, to very strict but loving parents. When she was just a toddler, her parents found an "early reading" tutor for her, who ended up being Merk. In this way, when she was small, Menzi put the ring of Frendall on her tiny finger and told her the spell.

Her parents knew everything about Isabelle's special role in the world. They were intelligent people who loved history, including the history of mythology and mysticism. Isabelle's mother was fond of combing bookstores for old books that might have secret, hidden treasures of wisdom in them. They were a believing pair, her parents, and because of this neither one needed to have everything proven to them. Because of this, the brothers had taught them everything about Isabelle's connections to history, from how the people had initially rebelled, to the destruction of Zanthar.

Isabelle looked like a heroine in a novel from an antique shop. Her hair was very long and dark—she usually put it in braids to keep it out of her face. She also often looked at people sideways with her penetrating green eyes, as if she could see into the minds.

Isabelle's parents were proud of their daughter, and they were particularly proud that she could fly, which had turned out to be her special power. They did have the good sense to keep her special identity secret, however. On occasion, however, this did prove difficult, because Isabelle loved to use her flying ability in public, pretending she was skydiving. She could fly so fast, in fact, that she had already made a tour of the highest mountains in the world, and had gone skydiving, secretly, from each of them.

Isabelle was an only child, and as such, she hated being alone. Happily, however, she had a friend. Isabelle had met Jonathan through Menzi, Loonce and Merk. They got along famously and often met to talk and wonder about the other ten children who bore rings.

"I don't know, they won't tell me anything." Jonathan would say of the brothers. But Isabelle never believed him.

They usually hung out together in the center of the forest where a massive, smooth boulder stood. Here, they could use their powers unobserved.

"When do you think we are going to meet the others?" Isabelle asked.

"We have got to meet them soon--just chill." The truth was that, deep inside, Jonathan always wondered the same thing. Are we the only ones? How will we find the others? Jonathan was continually asking himself such questions.

"We should get back now—it's two o'clock, and Merk is coming to tutor me at three," Isabelle said grimly, looking at her watch.

"On a Saturday?" Jonathan asked.

"You know him better than I do." She smiled.

They said goodbye, and Jonathan walked home. Isabelle, on the other hand, flew home. All she needed to do was just think about birds and she was off, flying quickly through the forest, feeling the wind against her face.

"Flying rocks!" she screamed through the air. She never flew all the way home but landed right on the forest's outskirts, just to seem ordinary. Then she walked home. She lived two blocks away from Jonathan.

"I'm home!" she shouted, walking in the door. Her watch said 2:50.

"Where have you been?" Her mother strode into the room.

"I was in the forest with Jonathan," Isabelle answered. Her mother sighed.

"Alright then, but did you see the time? It's 2:50. Now walk up those stairs and get your book and start reading." Isabelle's mother ordered her around like a drill sergeant.

"Yes mother," Isabelle sighed. Without hesitation she went up and began to read.

Chapter Three
Lina

Lina Kneel was born on March 3rd, 2000. Her eyes were blue and her blonde hair was bobbed to her chin and she was medium height. She had a very good life and a very kind family. The only thing that really disturbed, and even tortured, Lina, was the fact that she had to go to a horrible school where most of the girls were mean and made fun of her; actually, they did this to each other as well. The state of things made people sad and angry.

Her worst enemy at school was a girl named Rebecca Lebreckt. She was the most popular girl at the school and a real pain in the neck. Rebecca would always taunt her by saying, "Hey fool!" Or she would shout, "Hey Lina! Go get yourself cleaned up, snot!" The things Rebecca said were never true—Lina thought that she just wanted to exhibit her social power.

The worst part was that Lina had to put up with Rebecca in every class except for spelling, which was very difficult for her anyway. Lina was a very smart girl, but because of her problems, she was always sad.

But Lina had the very useful power of invisibility, which she loved. This power alleviated a lot of her sorrow and frustration because it permitted her to hide from

Rebecca and the others. Every day after school, she would go to a waterfall in a forest near her town. The peaceful beauty of the forest comforted her, and so Lina loved it there.

When she was newborn, Menzi had brought her a ring. Later, he appeared to her in a dream explaining everything about her powers and about another eleven special children who had their own special powers as well. These she needed to find.

"What other eleven?" She often wondered to herself. She wished that somehow she could meet up with them.

One day at school, Rebecca pushed Lina over the line of her endurance. Rebecca, walking right directly behind her to the history room, said in a loud voice (so that everybody could hear), "Hey Lina, I was talking to my friend over there, and I just want to know one thing: is it true that you have a crush on Michael Storm? That's what everyone's saying."

At that moment Lina slowly turned around and faced Rebecca, her eyes full of fire. How did Rebecca know? She wondered. Lina had never told anyone that she liked Michael.

As if reading her mind, Rebecca continued. "You're so stupid, Lina . . . you know that I could find out every little secret about you. It's so simple because you are so simple."

Lina took a step toward Rebecca. The entire hall was silent, including Michael, who was waiting to see what would happen next.

Lina stood facing Rebecca. Waiting.

"What're you gonna do?" Rebecca taunted her in a softly mocking tone as her friends came to her side.

Lina punched Rebecca hard, throwing her to the ground. She then pummeled her fists into Rebecca's face. All of Rebecca's fifteen friends just looked at each other in shock. One of Rebecca's most loyal friends, Callie, tried to pull Lina off, but Lina quickly got up and punched her too, chipping the girl's front tooth. Lina then continued to pound Rebecca until a teacher came out, screaming at them to stop and waving her arms wildly.

Long story short, Rebecca had to be hospitalized for a month, and Lina was suspended for a week. Lina could not have cared less, however, because all this meant was that she got to go and sit by her beautiful, gurgling waterfall with a smile on her face. Peace at last, she thought. Peace at last.

And the bloodstain was still on the hall floor.

Chapter Four
Michael

Michael Storm was born on April 4th, 2000. He had a ring just like Lina's, and knew just as much as she did about the other eleven, which wasn't much. Menzi had appeared to him in a dream as well, and told him about the rings, and that he would discover within himself special powers.

Menzi had appeared in dreams to all the rest of the twelve children as well. It just saved time and hassle. Plus, he loved dreams. They were just so cool.

Michael knew Lina at school; he was in her grade. He had always felt that she might be like him, one of the twelve, so he was in the habit of trying to follow her around. The only thing that got in the way of this was the fact that he was only in her math class and no other, and math was unfortunately at the very end of their school day.

When Lina had been suspended, Michael had been disappointed and even angry. She wasn't the real bully, but the teachers didn't get that. Rebecca was so mean; she should be in prison. Rebecca was just plain evil, in fact. Maybe it had to do with her upbringing, he thought.

But, Michael had seen a ring just like his on Lina's pointer finger. He wondered about this, and tried to get small glimpses of it as she walked through the school halls. Usually, he wore a fingerless glove in order to cover his own ring, so he knew that Lina couldn't have seen it.

Michael's power was to create storms, also known as *Atomikinesis*. He had made raging storms twice in kindergarten, only partially by accident. Those were fond memories, especially the lightening that had destroyed the tetherball post in the kindergarten play yard. Even as a small child, Michael had always enjoyed seeing the effects of his "weather work" on those around him, and especially on his teachers.

On the Monday after her suspension ended, Michael saw Lina at school, sitting on the bench by the front door. He approached her quietly and calmly, questions on his mind. But Lina just got out a book and pretended to read. She didn't want to talk to Michael. She had been horribly embarrassed by what Rebecca had said, and she didn't want a replay.

"Hey Lina. We need to talk." Michael's almost white skin was a shocking contrast to his black, wiry hair and blue eyes.

"I don't have a crush on you, now leave me alone," she said softly, still pretending to read.

"I know, and it's OK. It's not about that. Your ring . . . I have one like it."

"Very funny. Just go away. Is this a joke?"

"No, really. Look at this," he said while pulling off his glove. On his hand was a small, intricate, multi-colored ring that was exactly like Lina's. But Lina didn't look. Her eyes stayed on her book.

"Lina, please look," he urged quietly. "It's not a joke, I promise."

"Fine!" she muttered grumpily, putting down her book. Catching sight of the ring, she stared at it for quite some time.

Could it be that he is one of the eleven? Her thoughts were swirling.

"I can't believe it. You are just like me!" she said in shock. "What's your power?"

Smiling just slightly, Michael snapped his fingers and thunder rumbled overhead. Heavy raindrops suddenly began to fall against the school windows. There was a loud crack of lightening. "Would you like some hail?" he asked.

"Oh my gosh." Her face registered shock. "Do you know any others?" she said.

Michael shook his head. "It's just us two for now."

Chapter Five
Tom

Tom Clint was born on May 5th, 2000. He was a tall boy filled with wonder. His power was X-ray vision, but he didn't use it because everything got very confusing when he did. It was like he couldn't tell exactly where he was.

Because of this, Tom only used his power when it was absolutely necessary. Tom came from a military family. Once when he was fifteen he patrolled the streets of his neighborhood wearing a bulletproof vest, a helmet, and a knife and carrying an M16. When news reporters asked Tom what he was doing, he answered that he was protecting the neighborhood from stalkers and he would also help tip off the cops. If he should ever see stalkers, he would ask them to leave and that was all he would have to do.

Cops could not arrest Tom because he was not pointing the gun at anyone or threating them with it. Sometimes people would ask Tom to give up his gun but he would say, "I'll give up my gun when the politics don't lie." After a while the nickname peeping Tom lost it's purpose. (Eventually he got bored and decided to quit.)

Tom's parents knew about what he could do, but they didn't really understand it, so they didn't really discuss it. They also didn't know about the other eleven kids, because their son hadn't bothered to tell them that there were others like him. He considered that his dream with Menzi was kind of his own thing.

Tom had a pretty easy and straightforward life; nothing serious ever happened. He was super skinny — people sometimes called him, "the noodle." He was also very tall, so people thought he was older than his age. He had brown eyes and dark blonde hair. Tom got As and Bs in school, so his parents were proud of him and pretty much left him alone to do as he pleased. They knew him to be a good kid, not inclined participate in the crazy or illegal.

One of the only things that bugged Tom, however, was that on many days, when he looked outside his window over at the nearby forest, he was pretty sure that he was seeing something strange flying above it. Whatever it was seemed too big to be a bird and way too small to be anything like a helicopter. As he watched, Tom would try to zoom his eyes in on the object's location, but usually it would be flying too fast for him to get a good look.

After many of these sightings, Tom's curiosity overcame him. He decided that the next day, a Friday, he would go into the forest and find whatever it was. What or who.

The next day, Tom hiked through the forest to what he thought was the approximate departure point of the flying object or creature. He found a nice spot to watch from: a flat, smooth boulder on the banks of a small river that gurgled through the trees.

At first, Tom saw nothing. There were only trees, some birds, the forest floor, and some rather disturbing spiders. Suddenly, something hit him violently from behind, and pushed him at lightening speed off the rock. He hit the dead leaves face first. Tom swung himself over onto his back and sat up angrily. To his immense astonishment, someone was floating in the air right in front of him.

"Who are you?" he stuttered. "Or, what are you? Are you some kind of wraith? Are you dead or something?"

"No, dummy. Living. But let me ask you a question first, since you seem to be trespassing—how did *you* find this place? You'd better answer first." The flying thing turned out to be a girl, a very demanding girl that could fly. Now she lowered herself onto the dry leaves.

"I've been tracking you," he said. "You know, you can be seen from my window, flying around, from way outside the forest. Seems irresponsible. Shouldn't you stay *inside* the forest?"

She gave him the expert kind of grimace that all high school girls seem to have perfected.

Suddenly, something caught Tom's eye. He noticed that she was wearing a multi-colored ring, just like his.

"I have one just like that." He held up his hand.

The girl stared at it wordlessly. "Well I'll be darned. I can't believe I've met another . . . what power do you have?"

"X-ray vision," he said, then added, "I hardly ever use it."

"Well it's a good thing. Awkward! Wow. This is crazy." Isabelle shook her head in astonishment. They were both quiet now.

"What's your name?"

"Isabelle Dean," she said. "I was born on February 2nd 2000. Now what about you?"

"Tom Clint. Pleased to meet you, Isabelle whoever you are. I was born on May 5th 2000."

"We must bring you to Jonathan," she said. "I'm not sure what else to do. This is totally weird."

"Jonathan?" Tom wondered aloud.

"Our leader," Isabelle said. "You'll see. There are some things that you should probably know."

Chapter Six
Charlie

Charlie Lake was born on June 6th, 2000. He was the smartest kid in his class and everybody knew that he knew just about everything. He attended the same high school as Michael and Lina.

Charlie was usually carrying out illegal science experiments in the lab at lunch, however, so he had never hung out with them. (He had once in seventh grade accidently created an EMP and took out all of the electricity in his town while trying to resurrect his dead hamster. It took a full week for everything to get back to normal. Eventually he figured out how to cause EMP grenades, although unfortunately he could never get them to execute properly.)

Charlie was his own man, did his own thing, followed his own mostly scientific interests. And Charlie was pretty happy with his identity, that of a "brain." Sometimes, kids came to him with questions, which he didn't mind answering. His skin was light and his eyes a keen grey. He liked to wear button-down shirts and sweaters, kind of like an Oxford man. Questions were something that Charlie loved; he himself had many.

Charlie had also seen the fight between Lina and Rebecca. He felt that Lina's suspension had been unfair, since she had been defending herself against Rebecca's scathing insults. But, Charlie knew, just as every kid knows, that school is rarely fair.

Charlie's power was that he could talk to animals through his mind. It was also known as animal telepathy. Naturally, because of this, he knew tons about nature, the forest, and everything that lived within it. Sometimes, in fact, the animals would just come and talk to him, and tell him about their lives and problems. They found it entertaining to hang out with a human. The animals liked Charlie in particular, because he was a serious and patient listener.

Because of this, Charlie knew all kinds of things that he never could have learned in biology class. For example, he knew that female deer talk about how tiring it is to run from pursuing wolves, especially when pregnant, and how rats love the sewers partially because owls and birds can't get into them. He also remembered how one time he called an owl "The Bird of Prey."

The owl hated this so much that it called Charlie "Ape of the Hamburger."

Charlie hated this because he was a vegetarian and hated eating other animals. Once he went to a zoo and spoke to a lion. The lion told him that the last thing it had done before entering captivity was to chase down an antelope and rip out its intestines. Then, when it started screaming, he put it out of its misery by biting into its throat. It was all over quickly.

However, Charlie had other questions that the animals could not answer.

He wanted to know more about Lina and Michael. Ever since Charlie's birth, he had worn a small, multi-colored ring. It was strange, but sometimes he felt as if someone was trying to send him a message through it—it almost seemed to speak in a kind of invisible voice. Although it didn't make much sense, Charlie felt this that his unusual ring was linked somehow to Michael and Lina. But he didn't know how.

Ever since he had noticed them at school, Charlie had felt compelled to get to know Michael and Lina better. Are they just like me, but with different powers? He wondered. Michael and Lina just seemed different, different in the same way that he felt himself to be different. It was hard to explain, which also frustrated Charlie, because usually he was extremely good at explaining things. It was a feeling that he had that he could not shake. Could they also have powers? And if so, what kinds of powers might they have?

Charlie thought that maybe his pet cockatiel, Rain, might know something about them, so he went to talk to her. As usual, Rain was on her favorite branch, in her favorite tree. Unlike other birds, she enjoyed living in the forest. Charlie let her live there because he saw no point in caging her up. After all, they could speak to one another telepathically over long distances. When Charlie called Rain, she knew right away to fly over and spend some time with her master.

"Hey, do you know anything about those kids at my school named Lina and Michael?" he asked her.

"Lina and Michael hang out by the waterfall," she answered in a chirpy voice. "Do you have any snacks?"

Charlie was astonished. "Waterfall? Where? Seriously?"

"It's near the center of forest," Rain chirped happily, preening her feathers. "Other questions? Such as how am I feeling today, and what snacks I would just love for you to bring me?"

"Rain, not right now. But later. Thanks." Charlie was bewildered — for once, his head was spinning, just like the centrifuge he used for science experiments. Just as he began to walk away, however, his bird said something else.

"And you may also want to know that Lina disappears and comes out of nowhere sometimes." Rain said this mysteriously. Charlie felt his mind officially blowing up. He tried to approach Rain, but she flew off. "Bring snacks next time," she called. Weird, thought Charlie.

That Saturday he decided to go explore the forest more seriously than he ever had before. The forest was very large, miles and miles wide, but because he loved nature and could talk to animals, it didn't freak him out too much.

"Rain said it was near the center of the forest," he said to himself. "I wonder how she was measuring that?"

While Charlie stood on the outskirts of the forest, he tried to imagine what secrets it might contain. He had known kids who had dared others to go in, often at night; some of those had never come out again, or so the school legend went. Charlie had never really understood why kids would go in there alone anyway. He just had to find out about Lina and Michael, however, so he plunged deeper and deeper into the forest.

But then something began to happen. His ring started to pull him to a tree—he saw his bird in it, resting on a branch. Rain flew from one branch to the next, and looked at him, as if asking him to follow, especially if he had brought her snacks. Charlie began to follow her until she stopped and looked over at something very intentionally. Charlie followed her gaze, and thought that he saw Michael, in the forest, talking to someone else.

"Hey!" he shouted as he made his way over to Michael.

"What are you doing here, Charlie?" Michael demanded.

"More to the point, what are you doing here? Nobody would come in here alone unless they were dared, and I doubt that you have been dared," Charlie said. He pointed to Rain who was perched on his shoulder. "I'm not alone, and it's the same with you. So tell me, Michael Storm, who else is here?" Charlie demanded.

Michael gave a huge sigh then spoke.

"Nobody," he said.

Charlie knew when a person was lying; it was pretty easy to tell.

"Your eyes and voice tell me a different story." Charlie said this simply. "Give . . . it . . . up!"

"NOW!" shouted Michael.

Oh no! Charlie thought. Just then someone jumped onto his back and grabbed his neck. It was Lina.

"You would attack one of the Twelve?" she screamed as they plunged to the ground. Charlie knew exactly what she was talking about.

"I am one of the Twelve, you imbecile! Check out my ring!" Charlie felt like he was choking. He was running out of air. He threw his hand in the air.

"STOP!" Michael shouted, putting out his hand. Lina stopped.

Charlie got up, gasping. He choked out, "ARE YOU CRAZY?"

"What's your power Charlie Lake?" Lina asked him.

"Animals. I talk to them." He coughed. "What about yours?" Lina showed him hers by disappearing and quickly reappearing.

Michael clapped his hands and lightning flashed. Thunder rumbled.

"So, we're three out of Twelve. Do you have any idea where we can find the others?" Charlie asked.

"No," Lina said, "but maybe they can find us."

Chapter Seven

Quincy

Quincy Joyful was born on July 7th, 2000, and yes, her last name was truly meant for her. She was a joyful girl, but could be serious at times. She had curly blonde hair that reached just below her shoulders; her eyes were blue.

Most of the time, Quincy kept to herself. Her family lived in a great, grand house with three floors and many beautiful cats. Quincy loved cats.

Quincy's power was Identity Touch. With it, she was able to touch objects and people, and know everything about them, including where they'd been and what they had gone through. This power didn't end when she stopped touching, but afterward she could know where they were and what they were doing.

Her family had no clue about Quincy's special gift, or about Menzi, so they treated her like a normal girl. She went to the same school as did Jonathan Anderson, the first of the Twelve. Just like the others, Quincy often wondered about Jonathan, and felt a special, inexplicable connection to him.

Many times, Quincy felt that her ring wanted her to go and find Jonathan, and try to steal something from him in order to use her powers to know more about him. She even knew how she could do this.

Every day at school, they came across each other in the hallway while Jonathan was going to art and Quincy was going to computers. She also knew that he usually had things in his pocket that she might be able to pull out.

One day, during passing time in the hall, Quincy sneakily pulled something out of Jonathan's pocket. When she opened her hand, however, she found that she was holding a ring that looked exactly like hers! Quincy was profoundly confused. How could he have the same ring that she did?

If a normal person were to touch a ring of one of the Twelve, it would probably kill them, but if one of the Twelve did it, it would be far worse. Quincy let out a horrible groan of pain. Jonathan turned around with wide eyes. She realized that she had found her leader.

Quincy dropped the ring and began to faint. As soon as she hit the floor, everything went black.

"Quincy, Quincy, Quincy!" she heard, echoing.

"Quincy!" She opened her eyes. A circle of faces whirred around her. Off to her right, she saw Jonathan locate his ring on the ground, pick it up, put it on, and walk off like nothing happened.

"Quincy!" She saw a teacher making his way over to her.

"Hello my name is Dr. Raymond. Will you please come with me?"

"Sure," Quincy answered suspiciously.

Dr. Raymond escorted Quincy to the principal's office. When they entered, the principal was sitting at his desk. They sat down across from him. Dr. Raymond shut the door and locked it.

"Quincy, I think that I understand what just happened better than you imagine I do." The principal looked at her for a long minute.

The girl was silent. Her instincts told her that something strange was going on.

"Quincy, we know about your power, the Identity Touch. Yes, we sure do know all about it." The principal said this in a near monotone, but was watching her carefully. "We realize that this is a power that you could use to find out the material that might be on tests, as well as all kinds of other information."

Quincy was silent. She knew these people weren't going to help her. Chances were that they were probably going to try to kill her. Just then, she saw something red seeping out from under the closet door in the principal's office. BLOOD! Her head began to spin. Am I awake? She asked herself.

At that moment, she felt like her ring was trying to tell her to do something. Jonathan, Jonathan, Jonathan. The word came in a calm voice into her mind. Quincy had taken singing lessons and knew how to scream in a high-pitched voice, so she stood up in her chair and let out a shrill scream.

"Jonathan!" she screamed.

"Quincy, stop!" Dr. Raymond ordered.

"Let's do this the hard way!" the principal suggested. The two men jumped out of their chairs and tried to grab Quincy. She ducked and tried to snatch Dr. Raymond's keys, but missed. Taking her by the arms they pushed her up against the wall.

"We've death with your family, Quincy Joyful," hissed Dr. Raymond, in a snake like voice, "and now we're going to deal with you too."

Just then something happened. The door broke open and Jonathan rushed in. "LET HER GO!" he boomed.

"Hold her!" Dr. Raymond said to the principal. Then he turned to Jonathan.

"Hello Jonathan, I see you have come to save one of the Twelve. Well, she is a weak one isn't she?" Dr. Raymond laughed a shrill, nasty laugh that made Quincy's blood run cold. For a second it seemed like he was not even human.

"She's one of mine. You need to let her go, or I'll kill you," Jonathan stated flatly.

"Try me, Renmelion. The Ranian Empire will rule over yours like it did long ago," hissed Dr. Raymond. Jonathan charged him and pounded Dr. Raymond's chest with his hand. Dr. Raymond fell to the ground, his face turning gray.

"I can't breathe!" he gasped desperately.

"That's what happens when you try to kill one of us," Jonathan said with an angry grin. Then, he turned to the principal and placed his hand firmly on his back, killing him instantly.

"WHAT ARE YOU DOING? THAT IS THE PRINCIPAL!!" Quincy screamed.

Jonathan shook his head. "No," Jonathan said. "He is not." He opened the closet door, and the body of the real principal fell to the floor.

"He was a shape shifter. Almost none of the Ranian spies have any kind of powers," Jonathan stated. Quincy just stared. She was in deep shock and didn't know what to say. Ranian? Shape shifter? What?

"Quincy we have to go!" Jonathan told her. They walked into the main school office. The receptionist was slumped over her computer keyboard, a trickle of blood draining from her forehead.

"She was one of them. I had to," Jonathan admitted.

Quincy felt like she was in a dream, in fact, she was sure that she was. She followed Jonathan, since she no longer knew what to do. They left the school. Merk was waiting for them front in a lime green station wagon.

When they got in, Merk looked back at Jonathan and began to speak in a different language. Quincy, whose grandfather had spoken Welsh, guessed that they might be using a Welsh dialect. Then Jonathan turned to Quincy, and gently explained, "I am sorry that I have to tell you this, but your family is missing. Detectives are looking for them as we speak. Your house is completely gone; it appears to have been burned. Merk and I will figure something out. We are working on it. I'm so sorry."

"YOU'LL FIGURE OUT SOMETHING?" Quincy screamed. "HOW CAN YOU SAY THAT WHEN I JUST SAW TWO PEOPLE DIE IN FRONT OF ME AND MY FAMILY MAY BE DEAD? I NEED THE POLICE!"

"I understand you are scared, but you have to listen for a minute, ok? Just stay with me." Jonathan spoke in a measured, steady voice. "Highly trained assassins, like the fake principal and Dr. Raymond, are trying to kill us now which includes you. Those assassins got lucky. For now we're off the grid, but if you go to the cops, the assassins will break through their security lines and we will all die." Jonathan paused. "But, if you stick with us, you will be safe. We have unusual powers, too, and we can defend you. I know two more of the Twelve. One of them is Isabelle your cousin. Perhaps you didn't know. The others you'll be meeting later. But first, for your own safety, you need to come with us into hiding. We have a room ready for you now."

It still seemed like a dream, but somehow Quincy began to sense that she really was awake. She looked at Jonathan and sighed. Then it hit her. All at once she realized that everything was about to change, and that her life was about to become much, much harder, more complicated, than it had been before. She hoped that at least she would be safe.

Chapter Eight
Landon

Landon Harris was born on August 8th, 2000. He lived in a very big house with a lot of other people. He was one of nine children, and they all lived with their parents and two dogs. Landon was also one of the Twelve.

Life was not hard for Landon, although it also wasn't easy. His parents were quite busy with the youngest children, so he had to get most things done on his own, like get himself to school, make his own meals, and cut his own hair. Landon pretty much ran his life on his own. His grades were like Tom's.

More than anything, He loved to read, and he often read books out in the forest.

Landon had a mischievous personality that matched his appearance: his hair was short and brown, and his eyes brilliantly blue. Two of his fingers were deeply scarred, the result of an accident in his youth.

Landon's power was that he could speak to trees. He could also hear what trees were saying; he could even listen to the trees sing to him.

Actually, the trees sing to all humans, but no one hears them, only Landon.

He loved the trees' music; they sang songs he couldn't describe. He loved the forest so much that he would venture into it whenever he had spare time. The way he spoke to the trees was by playing a special flute.

One day, because of the love he showed for the forest, the trees gave him a gift: magic seeds. He found them sitting at the foot of a particularly tall oak tree, enclosed in a white, silky bag, which by some unknown power prevented the seeds from ever running out. If he threw these seeds onto the ground, they would grow into whatever object he was thinking about at that particular moment.

Landon took advantage of this gift. For example, he had once cast some seeds on the ground and thought of what he desired, and a brown cape took shape. It was a silky, beautiful cape that nobody knew about except for him.

He knew the forest well. He also knew how to climb to the highest tree near the center of the forest—it was an excellent of lookout. It was also Landon's favorite spot for reading.

As time passed, however, Landon felt something strange while in the forest. He could sense that the trees were becoming more and more concerned and agitated. They kept telling him about strange things going on in the forest: for example, a group of unknown people had taken to hanging out in the center of the forest, by a waterfall.

These people did not seem to the trees to be "normal" human beings. One of them liked to follow a bird around and ask it questions. One confused the trees by vanishing and suddenly reappearing. Another four liked to hang out by the rock; another evidently liked to float around in the air. The trees told him that all of these people seemed to wear small, multi-colored rings. They seemed to be part of a group, but what group it was, the trees could not tell.

Rings, he thought. Perhaps I could bring the different kids together, to talk to them. Perhaps they are other members of the Twelve!

Landon waited until the next day, a Friday. When the four o'clock bell rang, he went off in his car to pick up his siblings from school. Once home, he went straight to his room, opened his wardrobe, got his cape, and took off in his car, racing toward the forest.

At the forest's edge, he pulled on his cape, throwing the hood over his head, and dashed into the forest. He found a peaceful spot and played his flute while he waited for the trees to lead him to wherever the others might be. Eventually, he heard a song telling him to listen and follow. He twisted and turned through the forest as a trail of songs led him to a waterfall. There he saw the three of them: one girl and two boys, laughing and talking about who knows what.

Suddenly, a bird flew past Landon's head. Landon dove behind a tree. I'm a dead man, he thought. The bird spoke to one of the boys. After a few seconds, the boy turned to his friends and said, "Rain says we're being spied on by someone."

The other boy turned and called out, "Come out whoever you are, and we won't harm you."

That really freaked Landon. They were all his age, but he had never seen them before. Got to run, he thought, and dove from his tree.

"There he is!" one of them shouted.

"Get him!" yelled another.

Landon knew how to run. He was one of the fastest boys in his school. The sad part, though, was that these unknown kids seemed way faster than him, and easily caught up. Landon struggled and fought, but finally they pinned him against a tree. The girl and one of the boys each held an arm.

"Why were you spying on us?" the boy who had spoken with the bird demanded.

"I might know where others are," Landon answered evenly, testing them.

"Others?" demanded the boy.

"Others of the Twelve. I'm one of you," Landon declared.

"Look at his hands for a ring," the boy ordered; the other two searched him. When they caught sight of his ring, all went silent.

"He has one!" the girl said, amazed.

"What's your power?" the boy demanded.

"I talk to trees and have magic seeds that will grow whatever I might need," he replied.

They let go of him and he pulled out his bag of magic seeds.

"I'm thinking of three brown capes," he said. Then he threw the seeds on the ground and three brown capes quickly grew from the forest floor.

"These are for you," he said. Wordlessly, the three picked up the capes and put them on.

"Thank you," said the girl. "We are also members of the Twelve. I am Lina, and these are Michael and Charlie."

"What do you know about the others?" Charlie said. After five seconds he heard the tree's path of songs. Landon grinned.

"Follow me," he said.

Landon led them through the forest to Jonathan, Quincy, Tom and Isabelle. Once gathered together, they started making plans to find the others.

The ring bearers had noticed that they had all found each other in the same forest. For some reason, they felt drawn to it, as if their rings were trying to bring them all together. They decided that from then on they would divide up and search the forest each weekend for more members of the Twelve.

Jonathan, Isabel, Lina, Michael, and Charlie would form a search party and search for any others; Landon, Quincy, and Tom would stay and watch the central parts of the forest.

Chapter Nine
Marcus

Marcus Smith was born on September 9th, 2000. He always wanted to do what was ethical and right. He was a genuinely good person who liked to feel that he was following in his ancestor's footsteps. He never quite understood why he was chosen to have a ring and why he was part of the Twelve.

Marcus considered his special power to be a nice side interest of his, although it was by no means the defining feature of his identity. Nonetheless, Marcus' power was impressive: he could summon his ancestors to help him fight in times of distress.

Marcus hated the forest, which is why his friends always dared him to go into it. He had heard that very strange people patrolled the forest and kept others out. Because of this, Marcus avoided the forest whenever possible.

Marcus' family had emigrated from Mongolia when he was young. Like all his other relatives, he had black hair and brown eyes. He was proud of the fact that he was a black belt in the martial arts—he felt that everyone should know how to defend themselves in times of trouble.

The weekend after eight of the Twelve had made plans to find other possible members, one of Marcus' friends had dared him to enter the forest. Usually, Marcus never took dares. But this time, when his friends dared him to go to the center of the forest, he somehow knew that he had to go or he would be called a chicken forever.

I hate these bets! Marcus thought. Why go to the center of the forest? What is there for me to find?

The next day, Marcus entered the forest as his friends watched him.

"Good luck, idiot!" one of them shouted. The others laughed.

Why do I even consider them my friends? Marcus thought.

Thinking that he might need help, Marcus summoned one of his most powerful ancestors, a Mongol named Bold. His name meant "steel" in Mongolian. Bold knew how to fight; he was one of the best of his tribe. He carried a bow and sword and feared no man or animal.

Marcus spoke to him in Mongolian.

"Do you know about anything about this place?" he asked.

"Someone approaches!" Bold whispered.

"Who?" Marcus asked curiously.

"One like you," Bold said.

One of the Twelve! Marcus thought this over. Marcus.

"Three more are behind him, all dressed in brown capes, except for two of them." Bold said. He pulled out an arrow and readied his bow.

"These are not friendly. I must protect you," he announced.

"No! They'll think we're enemies, and they might be my friends," Marcus said. "I need them!" he pleaded.

Bold lowered his bow.

"If they kill you, I will tie their severed heads to the end of my horse's tail," Bold said.

Just then, five emerged from behind a curtain of trees and began to circle around them. Sure enough, four had capes on and two did not. The ones that did not have capes were an African-American boy and a Caucasian girl.

"Who are you and why do you have a warrior with you?" one of them shouted.

He realized that he had to tell them. He didn't have any other good explanations.

"I'm just like you," Marcus admitted.

They stayed silent, circling him.

"I'm one of the Twelve," he confirmed.

This statement made them stop and pull off their hoods. It was the search party that Jonathan was leading.

"Draw your weapons," Jonathan ordered the other members of the Twelve. In answer, the Mongol pulled out his bow, readied it, and used his best English "If you kill him, I will make you s-suffer from my arrows I will drain you of your blood, and your heads will adorn my horse's t-tail."

Marcus watched the other kids carefully. He could see them pulling out their weapons. Jonathan took out his gold sword, but then placed it on the ground before him. The others did the same.

"We mean no harm. My name is Jonathan Anderson and I'm the leader of the Twelve. All we need is to see your power."

Marcus pointed to Bold.

"This is my power. I am an Ancestor Summoner," he announced.

He then pulled off his ring and displayed it.

"He *is* one of us," someone commented, amazed.

"Should we take him to the waterfall, or to the rock?" Lina suggested.

"I'll check," Jonathan said.

He walked over to Marcus and looked into his eyes for a few, long seconds. "Waterfall," he said.

As the others approached Marcus, the Mongol raised his bow, pulling the arrow more tightly against it.

"Lower your bow," Marcus ordered.

The Mongol lowered it, but still looked alarmed. He walked through the forest with the others, not knowing where he was going. Finally they arrived at a waterfall. Landon was there, holding a white staff. He asked, "Is he Waterfall clan like us

"Yes," answered Lina.

"He needs a cape like the rest of us. His name is Marcus," she announced.

"What about him?" the boy demanded, pointing his finger at the Mongol.

"I am an Ancestor Summoner. That is my power. Bold is my ancestor," Marcus explained. Having heard this, the boy nodded, and pulled out a white bag.

"These are my magical seeds. With them I grew brown capes for all belonging to the Waterfall Clan. I'm planning to grow white capes for those who are of the Rock Clan, as some of us are. We chose to divide ourselves into two groups to make finding other members of the Twelve easier. Because there are twelve of us, we are going to form one more clan. Jonathan has chosen you to lead it," Landon explained.

"Jonathan said that I would be in the Waterfall Clan, so I guess that I'm one of you guys," Marcus said.

The boy shook his head.

"It was code. We need three clans with the same number of people, and we need you to start the last one," Landon said. "Now, what color would you like your capes to be?"

"Green," Marcus mumbled.

"What should my clan be called?" Marcus asked.

"Well that depends on what you identify with." Landon threw a seed on the ground and a green cape instantly grew.

"Thank you," Marcus said. When he picked up the cape, he noticed that it felt like very soft silk.

"Marcus, may I suggest a location for your clan?" Landon asked.

Marcus nodded. Landon pointed to the tallest tree in the forest.

"At the top of the tree?" Marcus asked, putting on his cape.

"Below it. Your clan will be called the Tree Clan," said Landon. "Marcus, I've climbed that tree. It is strong and friendly. Did you know that trees talk to humans by singing, but no one can hear them except me? That is my special power. Trees are noble and wise, and would be a worthy symbol for your clan."

Marcus thought about this for a while. The Tree Clan. I should do this. I can be a courageous leader for the Twelve!

"Fine, Tree Clan it is."

Waterfall Clan cheered enthusiastically.

Then Landon said, "Ok you'll have to go to Rock Clan and get the weapon from out of your ring."

"My weapon?" Marcus said shivering.

"Where do you think I got my staff?" the boy asked.

"The ground," Marcus suggested.

Landon chuckled. "It came from my ring."

"I could grow thousands of weapons from the ground, but the only one that matters is this staff because it came from my ring," he explained. "So, Lina and Michael bring Marcus to Rock Clan," Landon ordered.

Landon proceeded to throw a seed on the ground and four white capes sprung out of the earth. He picked them up, folded them, and gave two each to Lina and Michael. These were for delivery to Rock Clan.

As Lina, Michael, Marcus and the Mongol walked through the forest toward Rock Clan, Marcus noticed that Lina had two silver daggers, and Michael had a silver sword. He also remembered that the boy with the bird on his shoulder had a gold axe. He wondered what his weapon would be like.

Finally, they arrived at Rock Clan. The four members of the Rock Clan also possessed weapons: Jonathan had a gold sword, Tom a black wand, Isabelle a silver bow and Quincy had a gold wand.

Marcus noticed that the girl with the gold wand looked angry, as if she had fire in her eyes because of something in her past.

"Which one is Marcus?" Tom asked.

"It's fine, Tom," Jonathan said.

"Jonathan, please accept these gifts from our clan leader, Landon Harris," Lina said.

Michael and Lina gave Jonathan the white capes for his Clan, the members of which immediately put them on.

"Thank you," Jonathan said.

"So what is the name of your clan?" Jonathan demanded.

"Tree clan," Marcus said.

"Good, so we shall summon your weapon now. Is that correct?" Jonathan assumed.

"Correct," Marcus agreed.

"Walk over to that stone," Jonathan ordered. The stone must have had magical properties, for from it had sprung all the weapons of the Twelve.

"Point your ring at it," Jonathan ordered.

Marcus pointed his ring at it.

"Now say the word: I alw tiz," he ordered.

"I alw tiz!" Marcus shouted.

"Get down!" Jonathan screamed.

Marcus and Bold looked around, confused. Everyone was sprawled on the ground, their heads covered with hoods and hands. Just then, a shrill scream emanated from the ring and a bright light burst from it, blasting Marcus and Bold. They fell flat on their backs in stunned surprise, then lifted their heads, trying to shield their eyes with their hands. The light from the ring, however, was so bright that it shone right through their fingers and palms, illuminating the bones within them.

Just at the point when they feared that they would go soon blind, the light suddenly vanished. Marcus' mind was racing. What happened? He wondered. Then, he, and everyone else present, heard something hit the ground with a metallic clatter. The ring bearers arose and approached the rock: upon it gleamed a beautiful, golden, double-ended spear.

Chapter Ten
Ashley

Ashley Johnson was born on October 10th, 2000. Ashley's power was that she could scream incredibly loud, so loud that those around her were sometimes nearly made deaf from the sound. Her screaming could even shatter glass—the sound was like something not of this world.

Ashley was the best singer in her chorus class, but if she was not careful, she could also cause earthquakes and ruin people's minds with her screaming. Her friends called her "Banshee." Her family, however, thought she was a freak; her family members were also a bit odd themselves, however.

Ashley's mother, Gertrude, passed most of her time smoking pot and watching soap operas on television. She had once worked at the nearby tractor supply. She had once had a job, at the nearly tractor supply store, but had been fired after she was found stealing rolls of chicken wire for resale to 4-H kids at higher prices.

Gertrude would lie on the couch, hour after hour, letting the ashes from her cigarette fall onto the carpet. Ashley's dad, who went by the name Claw, trafficked drugs on the down low with a buddy of his while waiting to cash his welfare checks. Ashley also had a brother who didn't seem to like her much, Tyson.

Ashley herself had been in foster care when she was a baby. Because of a series of unfortunate errors she had ended up with Gertrude and Claw. While they did enjoyed receiving money from the system for her care, Ashley's family members treated her terribly.

Sometimes she thought this was because she looked different from them: all her adoptive family had blonde hair, but Ashley's hair was smooth, dark brown, and matched her deep brown eyes. Her mother's side, she had been told by the social worker, was American Indian, and very courageous.

Ashley's family hated that she could scream louder than the loudest train whistle. "You are a freak!" her mother would yell at her.

"You're an idiot! You're barely even human. How could you be my daughter?" Claw would shout at her. "Of course, since you aren't really mine . . ."

"I wish you would drop dead!" Tyson would shout without looking up from his Phone.

Ashley always found a bright side to her life, and she had great hopes for the future. One day her parents said they were going on a "family-fun car ride," which is usually what they called her Dad's drug "exchanges." This trip, however, would be different.

Where are we going? Ashley thought. They stopped right in front of the forest, the same forest where, only a few weeks earlier, Marcus had received a spear from his ring.

"Out we go," her father said in a nervous yet excited tone.

"What are we doing here?" Ashley asked. She suddenly had a very bad feeling about this outing.

"You'll see," her mother snorted. Ashley got out of the car, and saw her father remove his Glock from under his seat and point it directly at her.

"We can't stand living with you any more, so you are going to have to go," he said quietly. "Now get. Have a nice life. Oh, and any last words." It wasn't a question, but a statement. Is he stoned? Ashley wondered.

If ever there was a time to use her power, it was now. "My last words?! Sure, I'll tell you my last words! Ahhhhhhhh!" Ashley screamed her banshee scream. The sound was loud, long, and utterly piercing.

The car windows shattered and glass went flying everywhere. Gertrude's eardrums burst, and she keeled over, her tongue hanging out, in excruciating pain. A large piece of glass hit Claw on the head, knocking him out. The artery in his neck rhythmically spurted blood all over the steering wheel. The car siren went off. While all of this was taking place, Ashley was running for her life, straight into the forest.

Her brother, Tyson, had not suffered a major wound. He looked at his mother and saw that she was pretty bad shape. It looked like his father might soon be gone for good as well: face was white, almost completely drained of blood.

"I will avenge you my dear parents," he said calmly, looking angrily into the forest. He grabbed his dad's Glock and took off after Ashley.

Ashley knew that Tyson might follow her, and that he was able to run fast. She decided to hide behind a tree, allowing him to run ahead. Then, her plan was to double back, exit the forest, and leave the vicinity. Unfortunately, however, Tyson knew exactly how to find her. He crept softly through the forest, looking behind every tree. He was silent, the gun cocked and ready. When he found Ashley, he leveled he gun at her head from one foot away.

"You killed my parents with your power! This is the end for you my sister!!"

Just then someone quietly said, "Freeze."

Tyson turned to where the voice was coming from.

"Who's there?" he demanded.

"If you want to survive you should run." The voice replied. Tyson pulled Ashley in front of him and held the gun to her head.

"Walk away." The voice said.

"Prove to me you're real."

Just then, a silver knife hit the tree that Ashley had just been standing beside.

"Is that enough proof?" the voice asked. Then the knife disappeared.

Tyson immediately threw Ashley to the ground and began to run, but unfortunately he tripped with the gun in his hands and shot himself in the chest. He died immediately.

"Crawl towards me and don't turn around." There in front of Ashley stood a girl with blue eyes and blonde hair with two silver knives. Ashley stood up and said: "I must see him, one last time." Then when she turned around she threw up and passed out. It was then that Lina noticed the ring on Ashley's hand.

Lina and Ashley traveled back to Rock Clan with Landon. There, Jonathan explained the situation to Ashley, who all too gratefully accepted her new identity and summoned her weapon. It was breathtaking: a beautiful silver bow. Afterwards, they went to the tree where Ashley would make her new home.

Chapter Eleven
Nick

Nick Baker was born on November 11th, 2000. He had one younger sister and two younger twins--both boys--and he loved his siblings very much. He and his siblings secretly collected weapons (it was a hobby of theirs), and invented booby traps and other homemade devices. Nick had certain trade venues that he liked to use when collecting weaponry; it was all done on the total down low. Nick also often dreamt of being a rap artist.

Long ago, Nick had told his brothers and sister about the Twelve, and they had figured that if something threatened the other eleven children, they weren't going down without a fight. Of course, no adult knew about this plan.

Unlike his siblings, however, Nick had a unique power, which he loved: he was an Asteroid Rainer. (He had also told his siblings about what he could do.) Nick could cause asteroids to fall from the sky. First, he would look at or imagine the object to be decimated. Then he would hold out his arm in front of him, forming his fingers into a "v." He used the space between his middle and ring fingers as a "sight." Then, Nick would envision the asteroid falling. They always fell at a slant, for they followed the "v" of Nick's hand. This was how he aimed at his targets.

Nick could not call down any asteroids large enough to possibly kill the human race. The asteroids he could control were the size of small rocks about as big as baseballs, and even then, he could only make a limited number fall at one time.

Even so, Nick definitely possessed enough power to destroy his own town, or to do extensive damage to the nearby forest. Not that Nick would ever want to harm the forest or his town. It was not a huge town: the population was 60,000.

Nick's asteroids were legitimately powerful, however, and he could theoretically kill a person with them. An asteroid, carefully aimed, was more than enough to cause a fatal knock to the head. He always thought that his power was unique.

Although he was young, Nick had already had one unfortunate run in with the police. When very upset, which was rare, he would decimate mailboxes with asteroids — the smithereens would go flying everywhere. For this the police had hauled him in. Nick enjoyed knowing that he had some power, because often, like most kids, he felt powerless.

Nick had been brought in for questioning because he had been seen on the street of the ruined mailboxes; a local busybody (a.k.a. Tom) thought that he looked suspicious.

Answering the cops' questions was hard. He wanted to be honest, but the truth was stranger, in this case, than any fiction possibly could be. For every question that they asked him, he gave them three back. Because of this, Nick was not a favorite of the cops. Not at all. Plus, Nick guessed that they probably didn't like it when he spoke in his New Jersey accent, which was pretty much all the time. If you were to ask a cop about

Nick Baker, he would tell you that Nick never takes anything seriously and is irresponsible.

It was true that Nick sometimes got involved sometimes with school politics—"peacekeeping," he called it, also known as "pranking." On one occasion, the school bully, a surly kid named Brewster, decided to beat up a nerd that Nick really liked as a friend. One day, he saw Brewster standing on a ladder in the science lab.

The temptation was irresistible. Nick ran through the lab, casually nudging the ladder out from under the bully, and called out, "Hey Brewster, how's it hanging?" He ran. Fortunately, Brewster didn't see him—he had no idea who had pushed his ladder—and he still does not have any clue that it was Nick.

For the past month, Nick had seen kids wearing capes repeatedly entering the forest.

He noticed that one in particular was wearing a white cape; he looked an awful lot like a kid from his school. This boy's name was Tom Clint.

Nick had always been interested in searching for the other members of the Twelve. One day Nick's ring suggested that he go and ask Tom about the forest. He wondered if Tom might be the boy he saw in the forest, or even one of the Twelve.

After school, while Tom was walking, Nick ran up to him and asked, "Why do you go into the forest with a white cape on?"

Tom turned to him and said, "Who are you, the secret police? Leave me alone, jerk!"

Nick felt confused. It was very unusual for Tom to answer in such a manner. He was usually very friendly and rarely got upset.

However, Tom and Nick were also neighbors, so Nick would have more opportunities to find out more. It occurred to

Nick, in fact, that he could follow Tom into the forest.

That Friday, after school, Nick waited in his car for Tom to go to the forest. He leaned his seat back, so as to not be seen, and watched and waited.

Tom got into his car and sped away; Nick followed at a distance of about thirty feet behind to that Tom wouldn't spook and run. Nick had done this before, so he was pretty good at it. In the past, he had tried to find other members of the Twelve by spying on kids that he thought might be suspects. So far, no luck, however.

Nick followed Tom to his house and waited as he went in. Eventually, Tom came out of his house with a black stick in his hand and a white cape on his shoulders. He got in his car and began to drive to the forest. Nick followed.

When they arrived, Tom got out of his car and walked into the forest with Nick carefully following him. He ran into the forest after him. When Tom would turn around, Nick would dash for cover. When Nick was about ten feet behind Tom, he turned around and said.

"What are you doing here, Nick?"

Tom held a black wand in his hand--the end of it was pointed at Nick.

"I could be asking you the same question," Nick answered back.

"You had NO right to follow!" Tom stammered. He had fire in his eyes and his wand clutched in his hand tightly.

"I have every right." Nick answered.

"Leave me alone!" Tom screamed, he turned to walk away but then Nick said, "My ring tells me to follow you."

"Your . . . ring?" Tom demanded. Nick threw his hand in the air showing his ring to Tom.

"I'm searching for the eleven other people who have the same rings." Nick declared.

"Yeah well, you just found ten," Tom stated, his voice markedly less hostile. He walked over to Nick and patted him on the shoulder. That was easy. Nick thought.

"We must take you to Jonathan." Tom declared.

"Jonathan?"

"Our Leader," Tom said.

They then proceed to Rock Clan and Nick got his weapon, it was a brown Walnut wood wand. Nick was assigned to tree clan, where he met Marcus and Ashley.

Now there will only be one more left to find? Nick wondered. But who will it be?

Chapter Twelve
Rebecca

Rebecca Lebreckt was born on December 12th 2000, and obviously you've heard of her before. (If you think you haven't read Chapter Three again.) She had black hair that she thought was boring, which caused her to dye little strands of it red. Rebecca had also received a black eye during her fight with Lina. At first she had been embarrassed by her swollen, purple eye and had worn an eye patch to school, causing the students to call her, "One-eyed Becca." She wanted revenge on Lina, and she wanted it badly. (If you still don't remember, then you have a particularly poor memory for school fistfights.)

Rebecca's power was Telekinesis, meaning that she could move objects with her mind or hand without touching them at all.

Except for her ordeal involving Lina, Rebecca loved her life. Lina was frustrating, a boulder on the path of Rebecca's otherwise quite tolerable existence. Lina was the one who proved her wrong in quiz bowl, she was the one who was prettier, the one who possessed a beautiful voice, the one who had messed up her eye. Rebecca's envy of Lina had overtaken her, in fact, until all that Rebecca could think about was getting back at her. Every time she saw Lina, she saw the word "revenge." That word, in fact, was painted all over her life.

Nevertheless, Rebecca had become a popular girl in high school, mostly because she was wonderful at lying, and she spread unending rumors about others, Lina included. In fact, Rebecca had said so many bad things about Lina that not even her most loyal friends could keep count of them. She had all of her friends concoct unflattering rumors about Lina and she told them to spread them throughout the school.

The only people who wouldn't listen to these evil rumors were Michael and Charlie. Angry that Lina still had two friends, Rebecca had sent all of her own friends to look for their hang out spot; later, one of her friends had said that the two boys always went in the forest, somewhere unknown, wearing brown capes.

"I WILL humiliate them!" Rebecca would snarl. After school on one particular Friday, Rebecca drove to the forest; her goal was to hike into it and find Charlie and Michael. While walking, she reasoned that they might be hiding under the forests' biggest tree. By now, Rebecca knew Lina very well, and knew how much Lina loved trees and waterfalls. In fact, once, during an earlier time, the two girls had been best friends in middle school; once they struck high school, however, it was all over. Controlled by her envy, Rebecca made getting back at Lina her first goal.

Making her way over to what she thought was the biggest tree in the forest, Rebecca picked up a huge rock.

Watch out Lina, she thought. However, at the base of the huge tree, Rebecca was surprised to see what looked like two boys, a Mongol warrior, and a girl. The warrior held a small sword, and carried a bow on his back; he was dressed in robes that looked like they had been made from skins. *It's them,* she thought.

Rebecca stopped about thirty feet away from them, and hid behind a tree. Then, with all her mental might, she hurled the rock at the girl. But as Rebecca watched, the Mongol pulled an arrow out, put it to his bow, and stopped the rock in its course with a decisive hit. Then, the Mongol pivoted, pointing his bow right at Rebecca's hiding spot. One of the boys, who Rebecca could now see was holding a golden spear, motioned the Mongol warrior to lower his bow. He began to walk over to Rebecca. *Whoops, this isn't them,* she suddenly realized as the boy approached her. *I have the wrong people!* Rebecca's instincts told her to run, but as she turned an asteroid landed two feet away from her foot. Almost instantly, the four other kids were standing before her.

"Who are you?" asked a boy holding a brown wand.

"Rebecca," she said looking him in the eyes to show she wasn't lying.

"Why did you try to kill us?" the girl demanded.

"I thought you were someone else," Rebecca offered lamely.

"WHO?" asked a boy who was now pointing his spear toward her face.

"We're not in cave man times, so get that out of my face," Rebecca whined. "I was trying to humiliate three people, different people, not you; I obviously picked the wrong three, so you may as well let me go."

"She could be talking about one of the Twelve," the girl commented under her breath to her companions. I am one of the Twelve, Rebecca thought. She hesitated, and then blurted out, "I am one of the Twelve." They all exchanged glances.

"Prove it," said the boy with the spear. Rebecca held up her hand, revealing her ring.

"She is one of us, Nick." The boy with the spear sounded surprised. "Bring her to Jonathan." Nick brought her to Jonathan. Having inspected her ring, Jonathan gave her a green cape and her weapon, which was a shining black spear.

Chapter Thirteen
The Horn

Four days later, Jonathan and Quincy were getting ready to go into the forest for a meeting when Menzi approached them. He pressed a tightly wrapped green bundle into Jonathan's hand. "We're coming with you," Merk said, as he and Loonce walked down the stairs to the front door.

"We've made a list of all of the Twelve along with their weapons," Loonce said, handing a piece of parchment to Jonathan. It read:

Jonathan Anderson: Gold sword, Rock clan: Leader

Isabelle Dean: Gold bow, Rock Clan

Lina Kneel: Silver Knives, Waterfall Clan

Michael Storm: Silver Sword, Waterfall Clan

Tom Clint: Black Wand, Rock Clan

Charlie Lake: Gold Axe, Waterfall Clan

Quincy Joyful: Gold Wand, Rock Clan

Landon Harris: White Staff, Waterfall Clan: Leader

Marcus Smith: Gold spear, Tree Clan: Leader

Ashley Johnson: Silver bow, Tree Clan

Nick Baker: Brown Wand, Tree Clan

Rebecca Lebreckt: Black spear, Tree Clan

"Is this correct?" Loonce asked as Jonathan handed it back to Loonce. Jonathan nodded. The page symbolized all the combined powers of the Twelve; such information, in the wrong hands, might spell their destruction. Loonce folded it into his pocket.

"Ok then, lets go," Menzi said. He was already out the front door, racing across the street.

Menzi plunged into the forest. It was very unusual for Menzi to be acting this way. Finally they got to the rock where Tom, Isabelle, and Quincy waited.

" Merk," Isabelle shouted in greeting, and flew over to him.

"Hello Isabelle, have you been working on the Renmelion markings I showed you?" Merk asked.

"Tava," Isabelle said, which meant yes in Renmelion. Merk was teaching Isabelle the Renmelion language so that was why he was a reading tutor.

"Why are you here?" she asked.

"You'll see, be patient." Merk said.

"Jonathan, unwrap what we've given you." Menzi ordered. Jonathan unwrapped it; he found that he was holding a horn.

"Blow it," Menzi ordered. Jonathan held up the horn. It wasn't like a band horn. It was old, dusty, long and straight, and was inscribed with Renmelion markings, which read, only one of the Twelve can blow this. Jonathan held the mouthpiece up to his mouth and blew. Everyone covered his or her ears except for Jonathan, Menzi, Loonce and Merk. Jonathan wanted to stop blowing and cover his ears. But something forced him to keep blowing everyone didn't understand what was going on.

"Stop!" Menzi Shouted. He stopped and fell to his hands and knees. Panting and gasping for air he saw Quincy against the rock asleep.

What's going on? Jonathan thought. He could see Tom fall to his knees and flat on his face and fall fast asleep. Isabelle was on her back asleep to.

"What's going on?" Jonathan asked.

"They're asleep; you should join them," Menzi suggested. Jonathan tried to get up but was to weak and collapsed to the ground in a deep sleep.

"Let's go," Menzi said as he opened a dark hole just by looking at the ground. Then, Menzi, Loonce, and Merk jumped in.

Chapter Fourteen
The Dream

Suddenly, Jonathan was in a big black chair. He saw a jumbo screen in front of him; he was in a room of darkness, and to his left he saw all the other Twelve. None of them took notice of him. Then, the screen came on. It showed Menzi, sitting in a leather chair, in his room.

"Hello everyone. If you are seeing this, it means that Loonce, Merk and I have left. I must explain quickly. Renmell was not fully destroyed, and there are still people on a certain planet called Ellmar, which is currently three light years away from Earth. They need your help, for they must keep their king and queen on the throne in order for their world to survive. Here's how you get there: a portal to a space ship is waiting for you just five miles outside of town. In order to get to it, you must travel through the portal, which is a lake. Get your families and plan on how to get there." Menzi looked at the Twelve with an earnest look on his face. Then, the screen went black.

Jonathan woke, and as he did he noticed that his friends were getting up off the ground. He took a moment to get his balance then turned to his clan members.

"We must get the others," he said, and even before the words had left his lips, Isabelle was up in the air, racing toward the forest's biggest tree, and Tom and Quincy were racing each other to the waterfall. What will I do? They all look to me? Jonathan thought. I know how to fly the ship so all we need to do is get to it. Finally, they all arrived. They all stood in a line, waiting for orders.

"Okay, so what's the plan?" Michael asked. Jonathan clasped his hands together.

"Well we know it's just us," he stated.

"Yeah, because Menzi left us." Marcus said.

"He did not leave us." Jonathan stated. "He got us this far and told us what has to be done."

"Everyone, notify your parents that we are leaving; pack just what you need. We will meet back here in an hour." Jonathan ordered.

"What if we don't have any parents?" Ashley asked.

"Get yourself packed then go help another family get packed. Bring your biggest cars and be here by four." If everyone moved quickly, the timing would be spot on.

"What if we hate our families and don't want them to come with us?" Rebecca asked.

"REBECCA!" Lina shouted.

LINA!" Rebecca shouted. Everyone grew silent. Even Jonathan had no idea what was going on.

"We meet again." Rebecca announced.

"Why have you always been against me?" Lina asked.

Rebecca clenched her black spear with fire in her eyes.

"You said that you were goanna kill me!" Rebecca shouted.

"You started this, old friend, and you have left me to no other choice. " Lina pulled one of her silver knives out of her sheath.

"You can't defeat me," Lina challenged. "You couldn't at our school, and you can't now."

Using her telekinesis, Rebecca mobilized a huge clod of dirt and hurled it at Lina in one swift move. It hit her in the side of the face, exploding and splattering her with dirt. Summoning her telekinesis again, Rebecca picked Lina herself up off the ground and hurled her into the trunk of a nearby oak tree. Lina's body thudded against the tree, making a sick sound. "Uhhh." The breath was knocked out of her. Lina was

All of a sudden, a gray cloud appeared out of nowhere and it started to hail. Rebecca was distracted and confused by the hail for she did not know it was Michael's power. As Rebecca considered this dramatic change in weather, Michael quickly approached her. Quickly, he pulled his sword out and raised it high above his head: he was aiming for Rebecca's skull.

Using her spear, Rebecca managed to block Michal's sword. However, the fight was not over yet. Michael punched Rebecca hard in the forehead. After that, it was a free for all, as if civilization had suddenly suspended itself. Nick's confusion caused an asteroid to fall at lightening speed from the sky; it hit a tree and burst it into flames. Then Landon threw a seed on the ground that instantly turned into a giant mace. He seized it and turned on Nick. Luckily Nick had been carrying his crossbow, berretta and hatchet.

Isabelle realized that everything was going to break alarmingly soon. She decided that her best chance of survival was to fly into the tops of the trees and use them as camouflage. Charlie tried to help Michael, but Ashley, Marcus, and Bold blocked him.

Quincy decided to help Charlie. Turning, she attacked Ashley, tackling her and bringing her to the ground. The two of them grappled with one another, catfight style, fists flying. Tom decided to step behind a tree and watch everything with his X-ray vision, while Jonathan worked at calming everybody down. Eventually, however, he gave up that hope tried to wake up Lina. From below, Isabelle was filming everything on her cellphone.

In the midst of this chaos, Jonathan stopped and sent a message to everyone's mind: *Stop everything we know we are better than this. After all, our great nation must be united. A nation divided against itself will not stand. I will not allow this to happen.* He slowly raised his hand and a shockwave went threw everyone and time stood still for twelve seconds.

"Please, stop." Jonathan said. As time unfroze everyone stopped and Jonathan told everyone to go and get their parents and come back and everyone did.

Chapter Fifteen
The Portal

"Jonathan, what's going on?" Mrs. Dean asked.

"You'll see," Jonathan said calmly.

As soon as the families had gathered in the forest, Jonathan explained everything to them, and then asked each child to demonstrate his or her unique power. One by one, each member of the Twelve came up, stated their name, and exhibited their power. Michael created a storm. Nick summoned a few asteroids. Jonathan read the minds of several in the crowd. Then, he explained everything--the rings, the Twelve, about the powers. Strangely enough, all the families seemed to understand the situation, and few of them exhibited any shock.

"Come," said Jonathan. "Follow me in your cars and all will be made clear."

The families returned their cars. Isabelle gave Jonathan, Quincy, and Ashley a ride in her car; they were the first of the cars to go. Driving out of town felt weird, since they were fourteen cars all together, making all the same turns and traveling at exactly the same speed.

When they reached the open plains, Jonathan began to sort through his thoughts. Why did Menzi, Loonze, and Merk leave? What will I do with my kingdom? Where *is*

Menzi? Is he dead? He looked out his window, wondering.

After a few hours of driving, the sun began to set. Quincy had fallen asleep and so had Ashley. Jonathan looked out the window and saw a HUGE lake that nobody could miss seeing--and yet he realized that he had never seen it before. The train of cars stopped suddenly. Everyone wanted to see the lake; they walked down to it, following a tiny trail.

Jonathan was the first to reach it, even though the others were rushing toward it as well. At its shore, he gazed into the waves, and then stepped on something. Jonathan picked it up and found that it was a stone plate; the writing upon it was in Renmelion. The inscription read, "What is something you drink, you can't eat, and can kill you?" Jonathan almost laughed his head off when he read this question. Water, he thought, so bet that I have to say water in the Renmelion language. The only problem was that "water" was the hardest word in the Renmelion language to say, remember or pronounce. He turned to Isabelle.

"What is "water" in Renmelion?" He asked her.

"Dŵr," she said uttering the Welsh-Renmelion word for water. As if on cue, the plate lit up; gold illuminated its cracks and markings. The ground began to rumble.

"Get back!" Jonathan cried. "To the cars!" Before his eyes, the lake was caving in.

"Ruuunnnnnnn!" he cried at the top of his lungs. But none of the cars' engines would make a sound.

"THE CARS AREN"T WORKING!" Tom cried.

Everyone was freaking out. Even Isabelle was scared, although she could easily fly to safety--of course, she would never abandon her parents. Just then, Isabelle lost her footing, falling awkwardly. She heard the bone of her forearm snap. As if this weren't enough, right in front of her, the ground was caving in: the ground was swiftly receding, dropping away into a huge pit. Isabelle watched in horror as her parents fell down into this gaping hole. Not today, she thought. I started this, and I won't lose my parents by saying one word. With all her might she ran toward the hole and dove in.

Chapter Sixteen
The Shruut

Isabelle could see her parents falling as she raced towards them.

"Mother! Father!" she screamed at the top of her lungs. She could see them both reaching for the other's hand, although they could not see their daughter. Her broken arm made her feel weak and feeble. She watched in shocked horror as the groups of people around her also began to fall--to fall into the earth. She knew that she could not save them, even if there had only been a few of them. It would have been too difficult. It was all happening so fast.

As Isabelle watched her parents fall, the strangest thing of all happened. They vanished. She noticed that other people, also falling into the hole, were instantly vanishing as well. Nick, Landon, and Ashley all disappeared right before her eyes.

Isabelle suddenly understood that this must be the portal. It had conveniently appeared in the space where the lake had been, and was now widening, yawning into a huge hole. The sight was unforgettable. Now the lake looked like a whirlpool made of some kind of metal — if metal were somehow able to morph into a swirling liquid. She looked around for Jonathan. She knew that he would want to know as soon as the portal appeared.

By the time Isabelle had flown up and out of the widening hole, the cars that had been parked around the lake were being swallowed up by it; only Jonathan and Charlie remained within view. Everyone else had vanished into the churning, metallic portal.

"You have to jump!" she shouted to the two of them. The ground rumbled. Charlie's cockatiel was perched on his shoulder--the creature clutched his shirt tightly, terrified. Charlie and Jonathan were between the cliff and a car.

"JUMP!" Isabelle yelled to them. "It's the portal!" Jonathan shook his head; he had not yet realized what the swirling mass before them actually was.

"We're the last ones left!" Jonathan looked at her. Ten feet separated the two of them.

"OK, but you leave me no choice then!" Isabelle yelled. Like lightening she unsheathed her golden bow and shot at the ground right under them, trying to make it break off.

"What are you doing?" Jonathan screamed in anger and confusion.

"What I must," Isabelle returned. Just then, the ground broke under the two boys and they both began to fall. Isabelle didn't even bother flying. With them, she fell.

Isabelle's mind raced as the three of them approached the portal. The swirling mass sucked her in, and she felt a shock wave go through her body. It took her a few moments to realize that she was not falling any more, that the "fall" had been no more than a helpful illusion to aid in their transport. She found herself, instantly, to be standing in a white shuttle. Everyone else who had already fallen was there already, waiting. Menzi was also there, dressed in white clothing and smiling.

"Hello everybody," he said, "and welcome to Renmell's secret weapon: what you are standing in is called the Shruut."

Chapter Seventeen
The Twelve Doors

"Menzi?" Jonathan murmured, a puzzled look on his face.

Menzi continued. "So, as some of you have probably guessed, this is a battle cruiser. It can hold up to three hundred people comfortably. And we do have rooms and food for everyone: the dimensions of the Shruut are awesome." Menzi smiled in obvious admiration of the craft. "Right off, however, I need to speak with the Twelve, the ring bearers. The rest of you, please find your rooms, settle in, and be comfortable." Menzi explained.

Some of the Twelve looked like they were still in a bit of shock. Especially Lina. She couldn't understand why Rebecca had saved her. Her mind kept replaying the sudden appearance of the portal, the way in which it had sucked everyone into it, and the terrifying sensation of falling and falling into the unknown. It had been so sudden—the ground caving in and everyone falling into it. Not something that you do every day.

Lina remembered watching in horror as Michael had fallen into the vortex. She had tried to look for Landon or Charlie but Landon had already fallen in without her. But then the ground had broken beneath her and she, too, had begun to fall. But then someone had grabbed her hand. Rebecca.

Rebecca had held tightly to Lina and hoisted her up with all her might.

"Why'd you save me?" Lina asked as soon as she could make her way over to Rebecca.

"You are one of the Twelve, therefore I would risk my life to save you," she said simply.

"Menzi? How many people are there on this vessel besides us and our families?" Landon asked.

"One hundred people have been waiting here for two decades to help get you and your families to the planet safely. They are of a special warrior class called *Flines*. You probably don't know this, but right now our ship, the Shruut, is disguised as a comet shooting through space. We are traveling toward our planet, Ellmar, Earth's distant relative. We do have a foe: our old government. If it ambushes us en route to our destination, we will do everything possible to retain command of our ship. Merk is standing by in Armory and Loonce in engineering. This is, however, Renmell's best vessel," A sense of pride in the Shruut could be felt through all that Menzi said.

"What's with the unfriendly government?" Ashley asked.

"It's called the Ranian Empire, and its leaders specialize in overtaking other planets. They've waged war on about 30 billion planets so far, I think, (they specialize in assassinations and forced de-colonization), and we don't want to be added to the list. So far they have not found us. Right now we need to get to our planet without running into the Ranian Empire."

Menzi continued. "Here before you are twelve doors, one for each of you. When you step through them, you will be taken to specific sections of the ship. As an introduction to your duties as members of the Twelve, we would like you to make sure that your particular part of the ship is ok and run it. You have the skills to do this within you — you just don't know it yet."

The doors looked just like bedroom doors although they were extremely white and they didn't have handles.

"Stand in front of the door that has your name on it. When I call on you, push lightly upon it and you will find yourself in the station you are meant to oversee. We will start with the youngest member of the Twelve and end with the oldest." The kids looked at each other. It was alot to take in.

"Rebecca... Nick..." Menzi began. No one had any clue as to which part of the ship they would end up in. Jonathan's name was called last.

"You already went through your door Jonathan, this is the bridge. What we need you to do it to fly the Shruut, pilot it, home to Ellmar. She is strong and fast, but the hunter fleets of the Ranian Empire are always lurking, waiting for us to be less than careful." Menzi took a step back and watched as Jonathan grabbed the control lever and adjusted it to warp three; the highest it could go was warp eleven.

"We've made it halfway through a light year," Menzi announced presently. But then something dreadful happened. To Jonathan's astonishment and horror, a Ranian hunter fleet appeared on the radar as if out of thin air. Then, a signal began to come through. Menzi rushed forward to the communication panel and pressed a button just as, on a large screen in front of them, a man's head appeared. The man's face was noble and thoughtful although very fierce. He opened his mouth to speak. "Surrender the Shruut—

now—or we will destroy it!" the head proclaimed in a triumphant voice.

Chapter Eighteen
Six Not Three

"Whom do I have the pleasure of addressing?" Menzi asked the head on the screen in a very friendly and hospitable manner. He was apparently going to great lengths to appear very pleasant and kind instead of suspicious. Good strategy, thought Jonathan.

"Don't mock me, fool! You know who I am!" The fierce-looking man with the dark eyes stared hard at Menzi. His voice thundered. Suddenly, Menzi's own eyes bulged in fear. His mouth gaped open.

"Who is this, Menzi?" Jonathan asked. "Do you know him?"

Menzi, still staring at the head on the screen, leaned toward Jonathan. "This is my brother Venkian," he revealed. "I have not seen him in many, many years. There were once six of us, not three: Kofi, Venkian, Alaric, me, Loonce and Merk. That was our original birth order."

"There came a time, however, when Venkian, one of the eldest, didn't like how our country was being formed, so he argued with our oldest brother, trying to persuade him help him create a rebellion against Renmell. 'Who have you become?' our oldest brother, Kofi, would yell at him in frustration. And Venkian always answered, 'Don't mock me, fool! You know who I am!'

They argued with each other like this all the time.

Those two were the oldest out of the six of us, and they were also probably the most hotheaded. One day Venkian decided that he had had it with Kofi. He devised a plan. He led Kofi into the woods; we were there too, but we didn't know where we were going.

There, in the forest, three men with swords awaited us. "Is this him?" one of them asked. And Venkian nodded. The man pulled drew his sword and lunged at Kofi. Kofi was an excellent swordsman, however. He turned the sword on the three assassins.

"What are you doing?" Loonce screamed at Venkian. "What I must!" Venkian hissed. That afternoon, none of us had a weapon more powerful than the walking sticks we had brought on the hike except for Alaric, who suddenly pulled out a dagger that he had bought with his own money. Then, Menzi was cut off.

"That's when he did this!" Venkian boomed, holding up his arm. It was a stump of an arm, with a robotic hand attached.

"Alaric cut off his hand. But wanted to make us all pay, so he killed Kofi," Menzi said sadly.

"It was hard to pull me off of Venkian when I saw him award the assassins a bag full of gold. Alaric, Loonce and Merk finally pull me away. Venkian vanished, he ran off. Two days later, Alaric also disappeared. He said he was going to the market to get supplies — food, water, medicine — but he just never returned. Then it was just us — the three of us. We missed our brothers terribly. I was the oldest, so I tried to watch after the other two. We learned to stick together."

"Why didn't you ever tell me these things?" Jonathan demanded. "After all the years—now—I am hearing about your past for the first time?"

"Everyone has their secrets Jonathan. Everyone," Menzi answered softly.

Menzi looked back at the screen. "How have you survived for these thousands of years?" Menzi demanded of his brother.

"Easy. I took a potion much like the one you three took. Somehow, it had been made in Renmell. Even if we are known for our barbarism and not our intellects," Venkian sneered, and then, looking closely at Menzi, "Who's the smart one now?"

"You're crazy!" Menzi screamed.

"That's true, but now I'm going to kill you." Venkian's voice was chillingly cold.

"We'll see about that," Menzi answered softly.

"Order the fleet to fire!" Venkian told someone on his end. Then the screen went blank. A few seconds later, the pulse of a laser hit could be felt throughout the ship.

"Give me your sword!" Menzi ordered Jonathan. He grabbed it and plunged it into a barely noticeable slot in the control panel, one that obviously only fit a certain type of sword.

"Gofod ddraig!" Menzi shouted at the top of his lungs. Jonathan knew exactly what this meant. Space dragon! Just then a black hole appeared before them and a tremendous creature emerged from it: Rutia!

Of the three space dragons known to men, Rutia was the strongest. Each lived in its own black hole and possessed specific powers. Although, Rutia actually looked nothing like a dragon as we think of them. She was huge: twice as big as the largest Ranian spaceship ever made. She could wrap herself all the way around earth and, with a tiny squeeze, split it in half then blow it up.

Just then, a signal went off from the Ranian ship: an unmanned space pod was approaching.

"Open it," Menzi ordered. Jonathan let it through. Venkian had a satisfied grin on his face. Venkian held up his robotic hand only to reveal a button in the palm of his hand. He then pressed it.

"What are you doing?" Menzi asked.

"Launching seventy-two ICBMs at Rutia." Venkian grinned. "I don't give a crap about our older brother. All I wanted was to tick you off so you would summon that dragon. After all, we both know that is your secret weapon right? After all there are only two others and we already have one after all. A nation with no army will soon be destroyed. All you can do now is die." Then, the screen went blank.

Menzi and Jonathan starred in horror as the bombs penetrated Rutia's shields and blow her away.

"There is still one way!" Menzi said.

"No, it was my fault, I had to use it to keep the twelve from killing each other." Jonathan said.

"We can still get out of here and who knows what he's doing." Menzi explained. Jonathan put them on warp nine and they got out in a snap. All of the fleet was firing at them but the Shruut turned on its cloaking device and none of the Ranian ships could see them. It didn't take to long for two and a half light years to pass. Eventually they reached a planet.

"Ellmar," Menzi announced.

"This is your home Jonathan what do you think?" Menzi asked.

"It's the same size as Earth." Jonathan said. Menzi chuckled. It was true the planet was the size of Earth.

"There's eleven continents on the planet. We rule three. It's in a solar system with one sun and three other planets and has two moons." Menzi informed.

"What about the other eight continents?" Jonathan asked.

"There are two other countries that we've made alliances with, their names are Zerk and Benien and two of the continents are the north and south poles." Menzi informed. "The countries are powerful but we could take them down if they both turned on us."

"What's the technology like?" Jonathan asked.

"Middle ages." Menzi said.

"This is the one of the only pieces of technology we have so you'll have to get used to horses." Menzi joked.

Chapter Nineteen
The Thirteen Portals

"How do we get down there?" Jonathan asked. Menzi chuckled, and then pressed the "land" button. The ship was right above where Renmell would be. The ship dropped straight down and then outer space disappeared and Jonathan could see the bright blue sky. He really had no clue that the ship could go so fast; the next thing he knew the ship was on the ground.

"But how do we get out?" Jonathan asked. Menzi snapped his fingers. The next thing Jonathan knew, he was standing in a field facing the Shruut. He looked around and saw Menzi, Loonce and Merk standing in front of the Shruut.

"Everyone, welcome to Renmell!" Menzi cheered. Everyone else cheered, especially the Flines.

"Everyone, behold the thirteen portals!" Menzi announced, pointing away from the Shruut. Everyone looked away from the Shruut and saw twelve small portals and one huge portal.

"The big portal is for the Flines, who have come to rescue the Twelve." Menzi announced. "The smaller ones are for the Twelve and their families. It will lead them to the capitol building."

"Flines, you may go into your portal now," Menzi ordered. All of the Flines went into the portal while looking at the Twelve curiously.

The portals were very unusual looking. They had been made from blocks of stone that had been stacked carefully to make archways. Each arch stood eight feet high, and each bore a keystone that symbolized, in some way, the special power held by each of the Twelve.

"We will start from the youngest and conclude with the oldest," Menzi announced. Swiftly, lines began to form in front of each of the portals.

"Rebecca," Menzi called. "You start us off." Without a backwards glance, Rebecca and her family walked into the portal and were instantly gone.

"Nick," Menzi called. Nick ran into his portal in a snap with his three siblings so that their parents would have no choice but to run in after them. One by one, Jonathan watched all the other members of the Twelve pass through the arches with their families. I don't have a family, he thought. Resolutely, he took a deep breath and walked through alone. After him, Lina and her family passed through. Then it came down to Isabelle.

"Good luck Jonathan," she said, smiling at him. Then, she and her parents were gone. My only friend is gone, Jonathan thought. He looked over at Menzi.

"Did I go through my door?" he asked. Menzi shook his head.

"You're about to," Menzi said sadly.

"Come with me," Jonathan urged.

"We can't; we're not blood related," Menzi explained.

"What will you do?" Jonathan asked. Menzi shrugged.

"What are you going to do with your country?" Menzi asked.

"What Jelms did; defend it." Jonathan replied.

"You were like family to me, so thank you," Jonathan told him sincerely. Menzi blinked and gave him a confident nod. Taking a deep breath, Jonathan closed his eyes and went in.

Chapter Twenty
The Twelve Chairs

Jonathan exhaled and opened his eyes.

"Behold, the Twelve kings and queens of Renmell!" a voice thundered. All at once, Jonathan realized he was in what looked like a grand capital building; in front of him stretched a vast crowd of people all of whom were cheering and waving banners. He looked to his right and saw the others who were already bowing and waving like famous people, which they now, suddenly, were.

Jonathan couldn't say a thing—words were not enough to describe his swiftly changing feelings. In front of him he saw a throne. Gently, the realization descended on him that he was actually a king who now had to lead a nation: The United States of Renmell.

"My fellow citizens, I am here to lead you to triumph!" he shouted, pulling out his sword and holding it high in the air. The other Twelve followed him, and did exactly the same thing. Everyone was cheering happily, in fact the thunderous applause kept breaking upon the Twelve in waves and seemed that it would never stop.

After the introduction ceremony the Twelve were escorted to a large party within the capitol building. They were surrounded by masses of people wanting to ask them questions and clasp their hands. Luckily, each of the Twelve found that he or she had eight bodyguards to surround and protect them.

These bodyguards were actually Flines, a special class of humans who had been sworn to protect the Twelve even if it cost them their lives. They had all sorts of various weapons: Bows, Maces, Swords, Throwing Knives, Pitch Forks, Double-Bladed Swords, Blow-Darts, Shields, Axes, Hatchets, Spears, Machetes, Daggers, Clubs, Pike's and very few had wands. So, although many people tried to get to one of the Twelve, the Flines had them encircled. The Twelve's families were guarded by Renmell's secret service, also known as the RSS. In truth, the Flines were far better bodyguards than the RSS, but there were hundreds of RSS Agents all around the country and only a hundred Flines guarding the Twelve.

After twelve days of celebration had passed, the Twelve were brought into the Room of the Twelve. This room featured a long, rectangular table lined with five chairs on each side and one at each end. There were also place markers indicating where each person should sit—one marker for each month.

Each of the Twelve took his or her seat; they were waiting for something to happen, unsure of what to expect on this, their first day of ruling Renmell. Jonathan sat at the head of the table while Rebecca sat at the opposite end.

After a moment, a bald man, dressed all in black, entered the room. His build was powerful—the muscles in his neck flexed visibly as he moved, and his arms were quite large. The expression on the man's face reflected determination and the confidence of one who has fairly earned a measure of power. He crossed the room at a measured gait and walked over to a map that hung on the wall right behind Rebecca. Instinctively, she turned her chair around.

"Have you all been having fun?" the man asked in a serious tone. All members of the Twelve nodded. (Quincy Joyful nodded with especial enthusiasm, because she had gotten her family back. As it turns out, the assassins thought they killed her family by lighting her house on fire, but they had escaped out a back door. Then, the Flines had gotten a lock on her and her family and teleported them into the Shruut.)

"Good. I'm glad you are well." The man looked at each person meaningfully. "Sorry to tell you this, but play time is now over. Do you all understand that?" It was hardly a question. Everyone nodded nervously.

"Good, so let me introduce myself. My name is Brett Wetton; you can call me General Wetton. I'm head of the Renmelion army and as such, I have been assigned to you, the Twelve, as a special military advisor. With me, whatever Jonathan says goes." The man nodded briefly but respectfully to Jonathan.

"As you know, the nation is composed of three continents, and each continent has been divided into four states. By our reckoning of time, the year is 1437 A.B., meaning after the birth of Ellmar. Before the birth of Ellmar, the planet on which we now stand, time was measured by B.B., obviously, *Before the Birth*." He paused and glanced into the faces of the Twelve.

"Before we came to dwell on Ellmar, we lived in space. We came here primarily to colonize for our government, and to assess natural resources. However, our history has not been a happy one. Our government hid all of our spaceships, because the people didn't want to remember their past—namely, about how Renmell first fell."

"As generation turned into new generation, gradually the people came to forget their origins, including how they had come here in spaceships years earlier. They forgot how Renmell was formed." General Wetton pointed to six other continents on the map. The Twelve noticed that there was one island, up toward the North Pole, that wasn't labeled at all.

"What about that island up north?" Isabelle asked, pointing to it.

"That is the unknown island, the continent of Tenkrell," General Wetton answered. "Zerk, one of our allied countries, is having some difficulties with that island, in fact. There was a time when a number of disturbing experiments were carried out there—the government was even trying to create orks. They wanted to use the orks as soldiers in a new division of the military, the ZOF, which stands for Zerkan Ork Forces."

General Wetton paused, took a breath, and went on. "Their experiment backfired. The orks were given a chemical intended to make them behave like our own species. However, something in the chemical made the ork mind stop working, turning it completely savage instead. These savages are actually led by other orks who were not exposed to the chemical and are not savage. These are the most superior of all of them: they are called the royal orks."

General Wetton paused. "Needless to say, Zerk lost the island. The orks plan to strike the continents of Grune, Tamur, and Blention. Tamur and Grune belong to Benien, and Blention belongs to Zerk. If the orks, who we now call the Veltorians, attack

Benien, then it only follows that Benien will declare war on Zerk."

General Wetton was a man of great tactical skill. He was ready for just about anything, at a second's notice. He was also the only man who had the right to scream and speak emotionally in front of the Twelve.

"Ladies and gentlemen, we have to choose whether we want to break out alliances with Zerk or Benien, or invade the unknown island. If we invade, then perhaps we can find yet another of Zerk's scientific experiments: the Mowls.

The Mowls are also another experiment that went wrong, and are fascinating creatures. They are a combination of both owl and man. They look like an owl but have the shape of a man. They're built for combat, and consider themselves to be cultured. After Zerk created them, they rebelled, and took over the eastern part of the island. Later, the Mowls made a peace treaty with Zerk, and became allies with everyone."

Again, General Wetton paused and looked carefully into the faces of the Twelve, to see whether his message was sinking in. "When the orks rebelled, they took over all the island, pushing the Mowls to its northeastern corner. There, the Mowls built a wall along their border and around their capital city, using their most powerful weapon, the wand of Titus. (King Titus had been a great Mowl leader who died fighting the orks.) King Kalani then took the throne after King Titus died. The Mowls are now ready to take back their land. If we invade the orks, then the Mowls will certainly join our side," General Wetton informed them.

"How much time do we have?" Nick demanded.

"Two weeks at the most," General Wetton stated.

"The time is yours. I'll be waiting outside to hear what your decision will be," he said. General Wetton left the room.

"I say we do it." Nick said.

"My father was a marine, he would say this is a horrible idea." Tom stated.

"No, Nick's right, we should fight for the alliance." Landon said.

"Everyone, we have to invade," Jonathan said.

"But, we will lose hundreds if not thousands if we do!" Tom intoned.

"That's true, Tom," said Jonathan. "But if one conquers the other, they'll know that they can do the same to us."

"Those who choose to fight, please stand," Jonathan ordered. Everyone except Tom, Rebecca and Ashley stood; Tom had lost the debate.

"Good. Then it's settled." Jonathan said. He went to call in General Wetton.

"Have you made a decision?" General Wetton asked, walking into the room.

"Yes; we choose to invade the unknown island." Jonathan spoke as one possessing authority.

"Good. Then we must form an army," General Wetton stated.

"How many men do we have?" Lina demanded.

"Twelve thousand," General Wetton informed her.

"What about our navy?" Charlie asked.

"Out of the three countries, Benien has the best," General Wetton pointed out. "But, we have thirty-two fleets guarding our country."

"We'll send out six thousand men," Jonathan announced.

"We will also need some at home," added Isabelle.

"That will take three fleets," General Wetton stated.

"Then it's settled." Jonathan looked as if he were ready for battle already.

"How often should we meet to discuss daily affairs?" Ashley asked.

"I think once every two weeks should be enough," said General Wetton.

"Your eight Flines should be waiting outside. They'll come to you. And by the way, there are four extra Flines, but they are going to protect the capital building. If one of your Flines dies, then the others will be available to replace him or her," General Wetton explained.

"Go now," he said. Everyone went outside, including the Flines. Since the Flines always had masks over their faces and wore only black, no one knew who they were. Except the Twelve.

The families of the Twelve were already on boats docked at the harbor of Zanthar the Second, their new capital. No one had any clue what would happen when they got to their individual states. In particular, Charlie had no idea of what the future might bring; he did not understand why there were no birds, and he could not fathom what his own bird was about to become.

Introduction to Volume Two:
The Eleven Continents

Three years had gone by since the Twelve had reached Ellmar. They were handling their country very well; they were just and forward- thinking, and they always put the needs of their people first. In short, Ellmar entered a Golden Age. The bearers of the enchanted rings showed themselves, without a doubt, to be equal to the task of governing the country.

The six thousand soldiers had set sail for the unknown island.

Of these, two thousand were pikemen, two thousands were swordsmen, and two thousand were highly skilled archers. General Wetton had trained this army well with Tom, Nick, and Rebecca by his side.

Isabelle and Jonathan had married. So had Michael and Lina. Isabelle and Jonathan, in a surprise move, had been married in a private ceremony that the others had not even known of until it was over. Only the Flines had been in attendance. The Flines gave the priest who married them riches in exchange for his secrecy.

Michael and Lina, on the other hand, had a huge wedding that lasted three days. In fact, they even built a new castle for the event. From there, they governed their states and devised new ways to foster democracy and fairness among the people.

The other members of the Twelve involved themselves in new projects as well. Isabelle taught Ashley how to fly. She did this is by pushing Ashley off her capital building and screaming as loudly as she could. Marcus Smith, during the second year, volunteered to go off with the six thousand Renmelion soldiers. He took Bold, his Mongol ancestor, with him—Bold was delighted. Marcus also allowed Bold to bring his entire family. In total, there were nine Mongolians, eight boys and one girl. They were all willing to die for Marcus. Just like the Flines.

"We fight for no man but you," Batu, the only Mongol girl, said. There were eight boys. Bold's other brothers were named Chagan, Delger, Jargun, Jaran, Osol, Tabin and Temur, but Bold was the natural leader of them all. The Mongolians had been protecting Marcus just as well as his eight Flines.

Landon Harris was always out in nature although, when he first got to the capital of Alkrem, he didn't see a single tree. So, he got to work and planted hundreds of trees with his white bag of seeds, and then he got permission to travel throughout the country, planting trees everywhere. After he had reforested his own country, he procured permission from Zerk and Benien to go into their countries and plant trees as well. When Marcus set off to The Unknown Island Landon gave Marcus seven seeds to use one to grow trees along the up and down the west coast of The Unknown Island.

Ashley and Quincy focused on upgrading Renmell's technology. They showed the country's scientists how to make a light bulb as well as other kinds of light-producing devices. They also established institutes of learning that were free to all so that any desiring person, no matter what his background, could receive a first-rate education.

Charlie Lake stayed busy making new potions. He worked on cures with three of Renmell's best scientists. One of them had a friend who had lost his arm in a farming accident. The scientist gave him a revolutionary new medicinal potion, however, and in just a few days, the arm grew back even stronger than it had been before.

However, they had never tried experiments with birds. Charlie's bird was growing very sick and was going to die if they did not take care of it. They kept the bird in a glass room down in the lab under the capital building. Only one scientist could go in at a time and they were asked to wear a metal helmet while the others would stand outside.

"What are the conditions?" the scientists would ask, hoping the bird was in recovery.

But always, the answer was, "Not well, it's only a matter of time." That was always their conversation.

One day, however, the conversation changed.

"We need to give the bird the draught right now!" one of them shouted, who was in the cage, trying to keep the bird alive.

"We don't know if it's safe, Dr. Wood," Charlie protested. "Anything could happen to Rain."

"Do you want your bird to live? If so, then we must give it the draught!" Dr. Wood urged. "I'm hearing something weird." The bird was yapping a little, like a dog.

"What's happening?" Charlie demanded.

"It transforming into something!"

"No, oh no... I have to get out of here; it's caught the dragon disease!" Dr. Wood suddenly screamed. He started for the door, but by that time it was to late. The bird was already breathing fire and growing larger by the second. While the other three looked on in horror, she burnt Dr. Wood to death.

The dragon disease is what brought the dragons into existence long ago. One of the species had been found on Earth just as Benien arrived. It didn't live long. When it died, it let off a rare odor, however, and whoever breathed in the odor would be turned into a dragon. Even humans or orks could be turned into dragons, but birds were affected most of the time. The disease struck a note especially with those who knew about the chronicle of the Dinosaur Plague of long ago.

A potion was created that could heal the infected. It was poured into the eyes. On this particular occasion, however, it was too late for Rain. She broke through the glass of the exam room and stood proudly, a magnificent dragon. Charlie pulled the axe that he always carried off his back. *Till the death,* he thought sadly. He was about to raise up his axe but Rain had grown to the size of three pick up trucks stacked on top of each other. Charlie realized that she was going to shoot blazing hot fire right at him.

"Get down!" he called to the others, as he threw his axe toward the beast and dove to the floor. The fire was right above his head; he could hear the other scientists screaming. He knew that after a few seconds they would be gone.

The dragon flew towards the ceiling, which was at least fifty feet high. It tore through it right below the entrance to the capital building of Juung. Charlie got up and looked for his axe—it was about ten feet away. As he looked at it, he saw that it had become a mix of red and gold. He picked it up it and ran out of the lab, heading toward the roof. He knew exactly where the dragon would be. His Flines waited outside for him.

"What happened?" the leader asked him, seeing his axe. They were unaware that a dragon was on the loose above them, killing people.

"No time to explain, follow me!" Charlie ordered. The Flines were always by his side, running wherever he would take them. He found a ladder that was fifty feet high and they climbed up to the roof.

Charlie went first and saw that a quarter of the roof had been torn open by the dragon. The creature, which had once been Rain, wasn't looking but was roaring up at the sky. It was a cold rainy night, and the dragon was getting all kinds of attention. When Charlie looked back, he found that his Flines were right behind him; the last one had climbed up the ladder and had drawn his sword.

"Attack!" Charlie screamed holding up his axe. They charged, but that charge didn't last long. "Get down!" he screamed as the dragon breathed its flames at them. Everyone ducked, but two Flines fell off the building, covered in flames. By this time, a crowd of people was milling around below trying to see what was going on. When they saw what looked like fireballs coming off the roof, many scattered; others weren't so lucky.

"Get up!" Charlie screamed. He rose. His Flines still had not given up—at least those that were yet alive. He realized that the dragon was going to do the same thing over and over until she had finished them all off. There was only one thing left that Charlie could do. As the dragon shot its flames, Charlie held his axe out in front of him: it sucked the flames in. Then, he quickly turned his sword and shot them back at the dragon. The creature roared and flew off the roof. It was gone. Charlie just stared out into the dark night sky with his fellow citizens watching him . . . from below.